Natural Destiny

by

SHERRY DIXON

ISBN-13 978-1477675120
ISBN-10 1477675124

Book cover design by Book cover design by Cayce Morgan of Intuitively Artistic: Designs by Cayce. www.designsbycayce.com
Interior design by cj Madigan, www.shoebox-stories.com

Title page - Copyright Sergey Chernov and licensed from 123RF.com stock photos
Page 34 - Copyright Robyn's Nest and used under a Creative Commons license
Page 56 - Copyright Kobchai Matasurawit and licensed from 123RF.com stock photos
Page 124 - Original art by Raphael Unpingco, used with permission

The publisher is grateful to the National Park Service/U.S. Department of the Interior and the U.S. Naval History & Heritage Command for their extensive collections of public domain photographs. The publisher also wishes to acknowledge Wikipedia.com, Guampedia.com for making photos available under a Creative Commons license. For links to each image, see page 201.

sherry@sherrysdixon.com
www.facebook.com/sherrydixonbooks

Printed in the United States of America

I dedicate this book to my mother

and the thousands of other Guamanians

who struggled under the Japanese occupation

during World War II

Contents

Prologue

I WAS IN MY FIFTIES BEFORE MY MOTHER TOLD ME AN INCREDIBLE secret about her childhood: during World War II, between the ages eight and eleven, she was a prisoner of war on the island of Guam.

I learned this one Saturday morning when we were in her kitchen catching up on what had happened since our last visit one month earlier. Suddenly she stopped talking and stared out the window. There was a strange look on her face—as if she were somewhere else. When I asked her what she was thinking about, she told me about living in a concentration camp on Guam, something she had never spoken about to me or to my six siblings. Even my father did not know. She had repressed the memory, but as she said that day, "It's time to talk about it." And we did—for months.

At times I wondered whether the memories were too painful for her to bear, but she told me that our talks helped her deal with the demons that haunted her about the war. When she shared her memories, I wrote notes in a journal so I would not forget. After I had filled a couple of journals, she said, "Sherry, this needs to be a book." I agreed and began to write *Natural Destiny*.

I thought her experiences would best be captured in an historical novel told through the eyes of an adult remembering her childhood experiences. If the reader is interested in factual accounts and historical data, I have included a variety of links to information about the war and the island of Guam in the resource section of this book.

Because of the time my mother was kept in a fenced camp, she has never taken her freedom for granted. Because every move was controlled, she celebrates and exercises her right to choose. Because of the starvation she experienced, she savors and appreciates the abundance of food in her life. Because of the people who helped her have faith, pray, and recognize the good even when surrounded by evil and hate, she still holds fast to her belief in God and in her religion. Because she thought she had lost all her loved ones, she keeps family near and dear to her heart. As the second child of seven, I can attest that she loves with a magnificent heart.

My original purpose in writing *Natural Destiny* was to honor my mother. However, as I was writing each chapter and sharing them with the members of a monthly writing group I attend, I was astonished to find that many of them knew nothing about how Guamanians suffered during World War II. It was then I realized that this story needed to be told to honor not only my mother but also thousands of Guamanians. In the midst of the greatest adversity a child could know, my mother rose above her dreadful existence. She chose the good over the bad, love over hate, and joy over sadness. In doing so, she found her natural destiny.

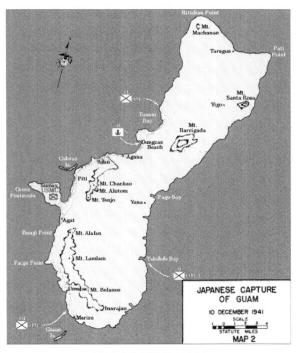

MAP OF GUAM, 1941

CHAPTER 1

Looking Back

I WAS SURE THAT GOD HATED ME AND THAT HE ALWAYS HAD—EVEN before I was born. Why else would my mommy die just before my third birthday and my daddy before my fourth? Before I started kindergarten, He took me away from my three sisters and my older brother. I didn't know what I had done to make God so angry at me, but it must have been terrible.

My name is Bernie, short for Bernidita. I am from Guam, a beautiful island in the Mariana Islands in the middle of the Pacific Ocean.

The original people of Guam are called Chamorros, but we are all Guamanians.

Not all memories from my young life are tragic. I have some good memories from my childhood. Some are about my Nanan Beha and my godmother, Nina Maria. *"Nina"* means "godmother" on the island and *"Nanan Beha"* means "grandmother." Nanan Beha was Nina Maria's mother. From ages five to eight I lived in Sumay with these two wonderful women.

Our house, the only two-story house in Sumay, belonged to the Americans. They let Nanan Beha live on the base and run her taxidermy business out of her house because so many Americans were her customers. For two years after my parents died, I lived with my Nanan Colsa, my mother's mother. I don't remember much about that time, but I do remember that she told me over and over again that I should never have been born. For many years I thought it must have been my fault that both my parents died. I thought that if I had never been born, maybe they would have lived.

Nanan Colsa told me that I should pray for forgiveness for my sins. So I did—morning, afternoon, and night. I didn't know how many prayers it would take to be forgiven or to find out why God hated me so much, so I prayed all the time.

Not all memories from when I was little are bad. My best memories are of my mother. I remember sitting on her lap. She had beautiful black, shiny hair that hung almost to her knees. Most of the time she wore her hair tied up in a tight bun at the base of her neck. When she wore it loose, her hair covered her shoulders and back like a black cape. Her eyes were the same color as her hair, and when she looked at me, I felt like she could pull me into her soul. Her hands were tiny and perfectly shaped to hold my body close to hers. Even now, more than seven decades later, when I close my eyes I can see her face and feel her warm breath. Her heartbeat was my heartbeat. She would leave wispy butterfly kisses on my cheeks and then wrap herself around me like she was sealing me inside her arms. I remember the last time she held me. I don't know how, but I knew that would be our last embrace. I was three years old.

I was Mama's sixth baby in twelve years. The day I was born, September 8, 1933, Mama was only twenty-seven. While she was pregnant with me, she was sick and weak; maybe that's why I came two months early. I weighed less than three pounds and almost died, but even then I was a fighter. My given name is Bernidita, but Mama called me Bernie because I fought like a boy. As month after month passed, I surprised all the doctors as I continued to gain weight and get stronger. By the time I turned one, I was no longer in danger. Mama could finally relax, but soon she learned that she was pregnant again and became very ill. She had had severe morning sickness with her six other pregnancies, but this time something else was wrong. She was tired and weak, had trouble sleeping, and rarely finished her meals.

Mama found comfort with my Nanan Juna, my father's mother, who came to our house every day to help. She was a joyful woman with a warm, wide, toothless smile. She was very poor; all she could provide were her ready hands. Mama welcomed them warmly. She adored Juna and looked forward to seeing her every day, not just because she needed help but also because she loved being around her mother-in-law's joyful spirit. I have vague memories of Nanan Juna playing with me and seeing Mama smile when she came to visit.

I also vaguely remember that no one, including my mother, was happy to see Nanan Colsa. The wrinkles on her face held her lips in a constant frown. She limped and walked with a cane. She was always unhappy and said mean things to my mother about how useless and awful she was. My two grandmothers were very different.

Nina Maria was Mama's dearest friend. During her weekly visits, she and Mama talked while Mama lay in bed; she was too weak even to lift her head. Much later in my life, Nina Maria told me that Mama knew she was going to die and made her promise to raise me and the baby she was carrying. Nina Maria agreed but dared to hope that her friend would survive.

Not long after that, my mother had my little brother, Manny, who was even smaller than I was. He lived for a few days and then went to heaven. Nina Maria often told me that children were special spirits that God sent to earth and that they always went to heaven when they died. Mama also went to heaven. I thought it was so strange that she was asleep in a box in the front room of our house and that our house was crowded with people visiting at all hours of the day. Strangest of all, Nanan Colsa slept night after night on the couch next to my mother. Mama slept in the box for almost seven days. She had always awakened before me and usually greeted me with a warm smile and hug. I didn't understand what was wrong. As I stood there waiting, Nanan Colsa woke up, scowled at me, and said, "She wasn't sick until you came along, Bernie. Now she is dead. We will never hear her voice again. She is gone forever."

Finally someone had told me the awful truth. Mama was not sleeping; she was dead. I would never see her again. God had taken my mother because of me. Shortly after Mama died, my father left home. After I had lived with Nina Maria for a couple of years, she told me he had run away to the island caves and had shot himself. He missed my mother too much to stay on earth without her.

For weeks after the box in the living room was taken away, it rained. The gloom outside matched the sadness in the house that seemed to hang in the air like a damp, dark blanket.

After Mama and Daddy died, I moved to Agana, another village on Guam, to live with Nanan Colsa. I tried to stay quiet when we were in the same room because she often told me that she did not like to hear my voice. I could not go in any other room except the kitchen, where I slept on an old crib mattress in the corner. I liked being in the kitchen because it was warm and quiet. My only visitor was Nina Maria, who came all the way from Sumay to see me. We were never alone when she visited me. Nanan Colsa was always in the room.

One Sunday about two years after Mama had died, Nina Maria came to see me. She usually came on Saturdays, but this time was different. She knocked on the front door, but no one was home except me. She came to the door of the kitchen and called out to see whether anyone was home. When I saw who it was, I opened the kitchen door.

"Bernie, where is Nanan Colsa?" she asked me.

"I think she went to church, Nina."

It had been almost a month since Nina Maria had last visited me. I was covered in dirt and was holding a chicken bone left over from dinner the night before. My clothes were ragged and filthy, and I was covered with infected insect bites. Even though I was five years old, I was not allowed to take a bath by myself. In preparation for Nina Maria's Sunday visits, usually Nanan Colsa gave me a bath, combed and braided my hair, and dressed me in a long dress, but she hadn't scheduled a visit for this weekend. No wonder I looked terrible.

"Bernie, when was the last time you had a bath and had your hair shampooed? Your hair looks like a rat's nest."

"I don't know, Nina Maria. I don't like taking a bath. It always hurts to have my hair washed and combed."

"Do you have any clean clothes, Bernie?"

"All my clothes are in the laundry. Nanan Colsa does not like to wash my clothes. She likes to wait until her sister comes to visit to wash my clothes."

"When was the last time her sister visited?"

"She came before your last visit, Nina."

"Are you sure, Bernie? It has been over a month since I visited you."

"Yes, Nina, I am sure. I get to help when my clothes are washed. It is my job to fold my clothes and put them away, and I have not done that since you came to see me the last time."

"Nanan Colsa does not take you to church with her, Bernie?"

"No, I do not go to church, Nina Maria."

As my godmother, Nina Maria was responsible for my spiritual development. Nina said she was going to wait until after Nanan Colsa came home so she could talk with her. After Nina Maria bathed me and fixed my hair, Nanan Colsa arrived home from church. I could tell she was surprised to see me all cleaned up with Nina Maria standing next to me.

Nina Maria didn't even say hello. "Nanan Colsa, it is time that Bernie come to live with me," she said. "You have done your part to take care of her and it is time that I helped."

"You cannot take her to live with you. People will talk," Nanan Colsa argued.

"Bernie is my goddaughter. It is my responsibility to take care of her and to raise her in the ways of the church. People will talk if I don't do what I am supposed to do," Nina Maria said. A few days later, I left Nanan Colsa and moved in with Nina Maria and Nanan Beha in Sumay, where my mother had lived and where I had been born. I tried not to look really happy in front of Nanan Colsa when we left Agana, but my heart was beating with joy.

GUAM SEAL

CHAPTER 2

Sumay

G ROWING UP ON GUAM WAS A LIFE FILLED WITH TRADITIONS. Any event was a reason to have a party. We celebrated births, deaths, graduations, confirmations, and other special occasions with traditional Guamanian food and music. A very special tradition in Guam is that each child is given a godmother. My mother made the right choice when she selected Maria to be my godmother. She was a hard worker, a natural entrepreneur, and a woman devoted to her family and faith. Nina Maria kept the memory of my mother alive by telling me stories about her. Nina praised me when I did something good and corrected me when I did something bad. While she was away at work, Nanan Beha took care of me.

Nanan Beha had raised several children during her life who had been abused or abandoned. Although Nanan Beha had a rough emotional exterior and anyone who lived in her house worked hard, everything she did was out of love and with an eye towards our futures. She wanted the children under her care to become strong and independent adults. As with the other children she cared for, I went to bed early and got up before dawn. Each morning and afternoon I did my assigned chores and went to school and church. Nanan Beha kept to this schedule, but she always had time for hugs and kisses, and yes, sometimes for spankings. One day she spanked me for getting too close to the chemicals in her taxidermy shop. When she was done, she said, "It hurt me more than it hurt you." That sure was hard to believe, but I did not tell her that.

It did not take long for me to adapt to Nanan Beha's routine. I needed stability, discipline, and most of all love—and absorbed them like a dry sponge immersed in warm water. I have nothing but happy memories of my time in Sumay with these two women who loved me. As my eighth birthday approached, I had big plans. Unlike other girls my age, who loved to play with dolls and with each other's hair, all I wanted was to run, jump, and climb trees with the boys. The summer before my eighth birthday I thought of a very special way to celebrate: I would cut my hair and stop wearing dresses. Each morning I spent nearly an hour combing and braiding my hair—time I wanted to spend playing outside with the boys.

On my birthday, September 8, 1941, I came home after school ready to transform myself. The house was empty. Nanan Beha and Nina Maria were both at church. First I unbraided and brushed my hair, a process that took me almost thirty minutes. My hair reached past my waist and was so thick that I had to use rubber bands and bobby pins to separate my hair into sections. The only time I had seen a girl get her hair cut was when Nora, Nina Maria's cousin, came over before she went to the hospital for ear surgery. As Nina Maria cut her cousin's hair, Nora cried and cried because she did not want to lose her beautiful hair.

I knew I wasn't going to cry. I could hardly wait to look just like a boy. After I sectioned off my hair, I took Nanan Beha's big scissors and I cut my hair until it was almost as short as my best friend Antonio's hair. I did not realize how much hair I had until I started cutting it. The whole process took me longer than I thought it would because my arms kept getting tired. I had to rest a few times before I could finish. When I was finally done, I could not believe how much lighter my head felt. I ran outside and relished feeling the wind blow easily through my short hair.

I cleaned up every bit of hair. I brushed off the counter, swept the floor, and then put all my hair into the trash outside. There was so much hair that we could have used it to stuff a pillow. I could hardly wait to show Nina Maria and Nanan Beha my new hairdo—but first I would do my chores.

I changed out of my school dress and into long pants and a t-shirt. Then I did my afternoon chores: sweeping the front and back porches and steps; washing, drying, and putting away the dishes; folding and putting away the clothes that Nanan Beha had put in the basket that morning. In less than an hour I was on my way to the church to show off my haircut.

All the ladies of the church were having a meeting to plan the Feast of the Immaculate Conception, a holiday we celebrated every year on December 8. Everyone was gathered in the community meeting room, a covered patio off to the side of the main sanctuary. I was all smiles when I arrived. At first, no one noticed me. Then all of a sudden, all eyes were on me. I was so excited that I had surprised them, but no one was looking at me in a happy way, and no one said anything. Finally Nanan Beha stood up. She was shaking and her face was red. She extended her arm, pointed her finger toward the road to our house, and said only three words, "Go home now."

I looked for Nina Maria. She was staring at the ground and for a quick moment looked up at me, shook her head, and then looked down again. I knew it was not a good idea to ask any questions, so I quickly left for home. I was sitting in the living room when Nina Maria opened the front door and entered the house. She usually dropped her things just inside the door in the front room and then sat on the worn rocking chair for a few minutes to rest her feet before cooking supper. This time was different. Nanan Beha was right behind Nina Maria, who had abruptly stopped at the door, uncertain of what to say or do. Nanan Beha, determined to speak her mind and not noticing her daughter in the doorway, ran into her.

"Go on into the house, Maria." Nanan Beha said after noticing Maria looking at me.

"Bernie. I was hoping this was a bad dream," Nanan Beha said as she stared at me.

I could not figure out what was wrong, but it did not take long before I found out.

"What have you done to your hair?" Nina Maria and Nanan Beha spit out simultaneously.

"I cut it."

Nina Maria looked up at Nanan Beha and moved out of her way when she saw her mother's tight lips.

"Go to your room, Bernie. Do not come out until I tell you. Go now!" I glanced at Nina Maria on my way to my room. She was still stunned.

Why were they angry? Once in my room, I sat on my bed, trying to understand what had just happened. Maybe they had both had a bad day. Maybe one of the customers had not paid them. But why would that make them angry at me? An hour passed before Nanan Beha called me to the front room. Nina Maria was sitting quietly in the corner of the room.

"Bernie, do you know why I sent you to your room?"

"No, Nanan Beha, I don't know. Is there something wrong?"

"Yes, Bernie. There is something wrong. Bernie, I am very angry that you cut your hair. On the island, all girls have long hair. Boys have short hair. It is shameful for a girl to have short hair. What were you thinking?"

I could not believe that Nanan Beha was so angry about my hair. It would grow back, after all. Unfortunately, I made the mistake of telling her just that.

"No, Bernie, it won't grow back. Do you know why it won't grow back?"

I could not imagine why. Was there something magical about the scissors that I used?

"No, Nanan Beha. Why won't my hair grow back?" I was mystified.

"It won't grow back because we are going to keep it short. For the rest of the year, we will make sure to keep your hair short so you can learn your lesson. You also won't be able to play with your friends for the rest of the year. You will go to school during the week and to church on Sundays and nothing else. You will do your work here at home and think about what you have done. On Christmas Day, before we celebrate the birthday of our Lord, we will discuss your penance again to decide if you have learned your lesson."

What would my life be like not to be able to be outside with my friends for three months? At least I would not have that long hair to bother with. Nina Maria did not say much, but that was our way. The oldest person in the room was always in charge. Nina Maria would have only spoken if Nanan Beha had needed her to speak.

It was weeks before Nanan Beha stopped being angry at me. Although I was not allowed to play with my friends after school or to take part in church social activities, my life hardly changed. Each day I still woke early, went to school, came home, and did my chores. Although I missed playing with my friends, I loved my home and my life with Nanan Beha and Nina Maria. Being restricted to my home was not punishment to me. This was something else that I did not share with Nanan Beha.

It was many years before I realized that although Nanan Beha honored many of the Guamanian traditions, she was an unusual woman on the island. For example, she had a daughter but no husband. When she found herself expecting a baby with no husband, she saw no reason to make matters worse by marrying the baby's father, a man she did not love. Instead, she took steps to take care of her baby by herself. She chose a career that allowed her to work at home and make enough money to support her daughter. One of her aunts had told her about taxidermy. With the American Navy base on the island, there was a market for preserving and displaying the native lizards, snakes, birds, and deer; the Americans wanted trophies to take back to the mainland. Fourteen years old and six months pregnant, she talked the captain of the base into allowing her to live in and set up her business in the two-story house.

For the next couple of months she learned the craft, including how to decrease her exposure to the toxic chemicals used as a part of the taxidermy process. To market her business, she prepared several animals free of charge for some of the soldiers so they could be used to advertise her work. It was not long before Nanan Beha had a steady stream of customers, most of them soldiers who lived right there on base close to her home.

Years later, when I arrived, she knew she could take care of me too. Though I was only five, there was no question that I would soon be helping out in the shop. Taxidermy was not easy. Some people in Sumay could not be around Nanan Beha's back yard when she was working on a customer's order because of the odors from the chemicals. I tried not to dwell on the uncomfortable parts of the job, such as removing the animals' insides. Nanan Beha told me that all jobs had something about them I wouldn't like, but the work still needed to be done. And besides, Nina Maria was not able to help because the chemicals made her sick. Early on, Nina Maria knew she was going to have to make a living in other ways. An excellent cook and a talented seamstress, she soon figured out how she would contribute financially to our home.

Nina's first customers didn't even notice the smells from the shop; all they had noses for was Nina's cooking. Her most popular dish was chicken *kelaguen*. She began by grilling chicken and chopping bite-size pieces of onions, hot chili peppers, tomatoes, and cucumbers. Next she squeezed the juice from a dozen lemons and cut the grilled chicken into bite-size pieces. Finally she mixed the meat with the raw vegetables and covered it in lemon juice. The delicious dish stayed in the icebox until the flavors had a chance to mix thoroughly, usually about two hours. The combination of the flavors made my tongue do jumping jacks.

Another favorite dish was chicken *adobo*. Nina simmered pieces of chicken and onion in a vinegar and soy sauce broth until the chicken came off the bone and most of the liquid had evaporated. The smell of the chicken slowly cooking in the mixture was intoxicating. Then she put the chicken and what little broth was left on a bed of white rice. Nina Maria had many regular customers who paid for the native cuisine. She cooked at night and then first thing in the morning delivered the food and took orders for the next day.

Nina Maria was also an excellent seamstress. For hire, she sewed buttons and stripes on soldiers' uniforms and did other minor repairs. American women, impressed with Maria's work, asked her to design and sew dresses for them. Nina learned that most of the American wives appreciated the bright colors and taffeta-like fabrics typical of the island culture. Reliant on and appreciative of Maria's services, the Navy let her use a closet next to the commissary for her sewing room. After delivering food early in the morning, Maria spent the day in her sewing room. When she returned home, she cooked for Nanan Beha and me and then for her many customers. She worked hard and seemed to love every minute. On weekends Maria helped older members of our church congregation with cooking, sewing, and cleaning. She also taught catechism classes at the local Catholic school.

Between the taxidermy business and Maria's two businesses, we were able to live comfortably. Other children who had lived with Nanan Beha in the past had helped around the house and with the taxidermy business, but while I was there, it was just me. It was a good life—even when I was being punished.

The three months with short hair passed quickly; after all, there was Christmas to look forward to and the end of my penance. Even though I was very happy, I still had a nagging thought in the back of my mind that God was mad at me. I could still hear Nanan Colsa blaming me for my mother's death. She never said anything about my father's death— but hadn't I caused that one too? I prayed each day that He would help me be a good girl. I also prayed that He would persuade Nanan Beha to allow me to play with my friends. I still enjoyed my short hair, even though several children at school called me a boy. But I did not care. It was worth not having to bother with it every morning and evening.

Before long, it was December 8, 1941, the first day of the Feast of the Immaculate Conception. Guamanians throughout the island went to church on this special day to celebrate that Mary had been born without sin and that God chose her to be Jesus's mother. I knew the day would not be perfect because I was still being punished, but I had no way of knowing that December 8 would be the first day of the end of my world.

THE FIRST JAPANESE PLANES ATTACKED SUMAY
AT 8:27 A.M. ON DECEMBER 8, 1941.

CHAPTER 3

The End of the World

BECAUSE THE FEAST TOOK PLACE ON A MONDAY, THERE WAS NO school. After morning Mass, everyone gathered outside the church for a huge feast, island music, and dancing. On my way to church that morning, I had noticed a pig and several chickens cooking on the rotisserie in the church's back yard. I could also smell pork, beef ribs, and fish. Nina Maria must have cooked those earlier that morning on the same grills. Next to the church playground four picnic tables were filled with chicken and cheese empanadas, fried rice, Spanish rice, fruit salads and all kinds of desserts, including fermented coconut candy (*ahu*), chocolate cake, custard éclairs, and Guamanian pudding made with real vanilla and bananas.

I had trouble concentrating during the one-hour Mass, though I did enjoy listening to the choir's rich harmonies. As soon as Mass ended, Nanan Beha told me to leave for home. Under normal circumstances I would have stayed at the church to celebrate, but I was still being punished for cutting my hair. I would miss the delicious food and the singing accompanied by ukuleles and guitars. And Uncle Mong, the oldest man in the village, was going to play his harmonica!

I started the long walk home, sadness my only companion. Soon the music and laughter grew faint, and I could no longer smell the feast. Arriving home, I walked through the front door. As my eyes filled with tears, I closed the door and walked into my bedroom. Feeling the punishment was too harsh, I threw myself down on my bed and buried my face in my pillow. Knowing that feeling sorry for myself was not going to get me back to the celebration, I sat up and went into the kitchen to start my list of chores. Determined to get everything done on Nanan Beha's list, I picked up the broom and hoped that my punishment would be lightened if I did a really good job.

All of a sudden, a horrible booming noise shook the house. What was it? I had never heard anything like it before. The deafening sound was not coming from inside the house. It was from outside. I threw the broom down, ran to the front door, pulled it open, and could not believe what I saw. People were screaming, crying, running, bleeding, and collapsing. What had happened? Was it a typhoon? An earthquake? Homes were on fire and the sky was full of smoke. As I stared at the scene, I saw streaks of fire race through the sky, land on the ground, and then explode.

Bombs! These were bombs! We had discussed them in our social studies class at school. Miss Salas, my teacher, had invited one of the Americans to talk to our class. He brought pictures of bombs exploding and all the damage they could do. The scene outside my home looked just like the pictures he had brought to school. Bombs were dropping from the sky, destroying everything for miles. I could see that most were landing next to the Standard Oil tank one mile away. My head felt like it was going to burst from the sound of the explosions. The thick smoke, fire-hot debris, and smell of burning flesh bombarded my senses. I had never heard such screams of terror and pain. I could see that my church, which I loved as much as I loved my home and where minutes before I had left my friends and family, had been reduced to rubble. I wanted to wake up from the terrible nightmare but knew I was not asleep. My little Catholic church, my friends, my dear Nanan Beha, and my sweet Nina Maria were gone.

Finally the bombing stopped. Instinctively I knew the break in the horror was only temporary. I lowered my hands, which I had pressed against my ears to protect them from the onslaught of noise. There was no color left anywhere except for the orange fires, which were everywhere. My beautiful tropical island—usually splashed with the bright colors of flowers, tropical birds, and palm trees—was reduced to black and gray. In minutes, life had been replaced by death. All around I saw people lying on the ground. Some were unrecognizable—their arms, heads, and legs blown off and scattered to the wind. Men and women staggered in shock and confusion. Crying children walked aimlessly with no one by their side.

My eyes were wide with fear as I stood paralyzed on my front porch. I was released from my own fear when I noticed a man stumbling towards me, his face contorted with pain and covered with blood. I did not recognize him. He had been hit with what looked like a jagged piece of metal that was still buried in his chest.

"Help me, help me!" he cried as he moved toward me.

I was terrified. Under normal circumstances, I would have reached out to help anyone in need, but these were not normal circumstances. I turned back into the house and slammed the door, trying to erase the horror. As soon as I collapsed onto the couch, airplanes returned overhead with more bombs. Instinctively I started looking for something in the front room. I was not sure what it was, but somehow I knew I would find it. As I lifted the couch cushions, I could hear the man on the front porch.

"Help me! Please help me!" The man continued to cry out, but I did nothing to help.

Then I saw it—the something for which I had been searching: my little statue of the Virgin Mary. After my mother died, the statue that she had kept on her nightstand was all I had left of her. I cradled it in my arms, ran into my bedroom, closed the door, and hurriedly slid under the bed, with Mary tucked close to my chest, protecting me.

I remained under the bed, praying for the bombing to stop. Several hours later when I emerged, daylight was streaming through the windows. The bombing had stopped, but there were no recognizable sounds coming from the street outside. There was only soft whimpering, moaning, and crying from the island people outside.

I opened the bedroom door and saw that the injured man had come into my house. He was lying on the couch, not moving. His skin was a strange gray color. I had never seen a dead person before, but I knew one was in my living room. I felt nauseated and ran to the door to throw up.

I was afraid, but not because there was a dead man on the floor of my house and his blood was turning Nanan Beha's sage green rug a horrible reddish-brown.

I was afraid, but not because when I had opened the door to the street, I saw destruction of my once peaceful community.

I was afraid, but not because I had lost my family and saw no one I knew amidst the horror as I walked slowly into the street swept along with the other survivors.

I was afraid because, as I was being pulled along with the crowd heading toward the safety of the island caves, I seemed to have no feelings at all.

A CAVE IN THE FENA RESERVOIR AREA

CHAPTER 4

Sanctuary

THE SUN WAS SETTING—NORMALLY MY SECOND FAVORITE PART OF the day. My most favorite was the early morning, when Nanan Beha and I enjoyed sitting in silence. She rose every morning around 4:30. She loved to sit and rock in the quiet and not say a word while soaking in the early morning. I would take my place on the bottom step of the porch and enjoy this special time with her. She used to say that this was when nature's real work went on. The night animals would say their final goodbyes and some, like Mr. Snake, would slither off into the jungle, the moon reflecting on his scales. Nanan Beha and I sat peacefully, our soft voices intruders in the world of night animals. I loved her more at this time than any other. Now I realized I would never see her again.

I tried not to cry, but the tears would not stop. Though I was surrounded by people, I was alone as I walked away from the two-story house on a dirt road, along with hundreds of other people. At first I did not know where we were going, just that we were all walking in the same direction. Most of my village had been destroyed. The only landmark I recognized besides my home, which had been miraculously spared, was the five-foot cross outside our little Catholic church; it stood firm like a fist in the face of the Japanese bombs.

It was not difficult for me to leave my home. When I turned to look at the remains of the village, there was nothing left that looked like home. My friend Antonio's house, now a pile of ashes, had once been just across the street. Was it just this morning that I had waved to Antonio as he left to attend Mass? Was it just a few hours ago that I had passed by his house, watching as his grandfather left for the feast? Was there really ever a house in that spot? Had there ever been a village?

Three years earlier I had walked alongside Nina Maria toward Nanan Beha's house for the first time on this same road. It was a long hot walk; the sun warmed our bare heads. I didn't care that it was hot. I loved being outside. When I lived with Nanan Colsa, I was rarely allowed to go outside. I spent most of the time in the corner of the kitchen, out of the way.

Nanan Colsa paid little attention to me, but I did not mind because her company was so unpleasant. I liked being by myself in the kitchen. The food was cooked outside, right next to the open kitchen door, on open fires. Most of Nanan Colsa's visitors were old and did not even notice me. I remember only one visitor, Nina Maria. When she came, I was the center of her world. During her visits she told me stories about my mother and reminded me how much Mama enjoyed brushing my hair and making me laugh. Soon I could recall only a few details about her. One morning when I was five, Nina Maria arrived in Agana for her visit. She began telling me a story about Mama, when Nanan Colsa interrupted.

"Caridad was a useless woman," she said. "All she knew was how to be pregnant. Look what she left behind—a litter of children."

Nina Maria did not respond to Nanan Colsa—very few people talked back to an elder. Nanan Colsa, a chronic tobacco chewer, ended the conversation by spitting into the nearest wastebasket and telling Nina Maria to leave. However, the next time Nina Maria visited was different.

The next time Maria visited, which was several weeks later, was the visit that changed my life. That was the day she persuaded Nanan Colsa to let me live in Sumay. I held her hand, my smile as broad as the horizon at the edge of the ocean as we started the seven-mile walk from Agana to my new home. I did not care how long we had to walk. I was going to start a new life.

This time as I walked toward the caves, I closed my eyes, trying to squeeze out the present and slip back to the past. I envisioned the day Nina Maria and I opened the door to my new home. Nanan Beha was on the porch. Her arms were crossed, but she had a gentle smile on her face.

"What do we have here, Maria?" Nanan Beha asked.

"Bernie has come to live with us at last," Nina Maria said, as she helped me up the stairs.

"She looks like she has been rolling around in the dirt, playing with animal dung. Let's get her bathed."

Nanan Beha and Nina Maria scrubbed me until they found the soft brown skin beneath the layers of dirt. Then there was my hair to deal with; it was infested with lice.

"Perhaps we ought to cut her hair, Nanan Beha. We cannot rid her of the lice with this head full of thick hair," Nina pleaded.

"Island girls do not cut their hair, Maria. You know that. We will not shame her in that way. We will comb each hair until we remove all of the little pests." She was true to her word. After five hours my hair was fresh and clean—and still long.

Nanan Beha set about making a schedule for me. Each day when I awoke, I made my bed. Then I kneeled and thanked my Lord Jesus Christ for giving me a loving home. Next I brought water from the nearby stream to the kitchen and put a pot of water on the stove to boil. Nanan Beha did not splurge on much, but she always made sure there was coffee. Nina Maria had many American soldier friends who always had time to share a cup of morning coffee with me and Nanan

Beha. Coffee soon became my favorite drink.

Early each morning, after finishing the last minute details for the food orders she had cooked the night before, Nina Maria left home to drop off the food to her customers on her way to work. Although most days I did not see her until just before bedtime, I always felt her presence.

But now, all alone, I could not feel anything. I opened my eyes and saw once again that my quiet, wonderful life had been destroyed. Now I was walking on a familiar road in an unfamiliar scene with the other Sumay survivors toward the sanctuary of the island caves. I knew someone would take care of me because it was the island way. I should have taken some comfort in knowing that, but I did not.

I yearned for my routine. I should have been finishing my chores by now. Nanan Beha would have been arriving home from Mass. It was such a short time ago, wasn't it, that I had wished that soft-hearted Nanan Beha would reduce her punishment and allow me to enjoy the evening festivities at the church. After attending evening Mass and waiting for the festivities to end, I should have been brushing my teeth and hair and then kneeling at my bed, giving thanks for the events of the day.

Now there was nothing to be thankful for. Instead I was walking away from the village, watching every step to avoid stepping on an arm or leg or head, knowing I would never again feel Nanan Beha's gentle touch or hear Nina Maria's angelic voice.

My feet grew heavier as sadness filled my heart. We continued to walk toward the island caves, where we would be safe. We had always gone there to escape danger—mostly Mother Nature's furious storms. The two-mile walk seemed to take days instead of hours. I was exhausted and hungry, but it would be a long time before we would be able to rest or eat. As I was drowning in hopelessness, a woman came to walk alongside of me. Her hair was black with streaks of silver throughout. She was wearing a silver necklace with a pearl white cross at the end.

"Where are your people? Do you know?" she asked me, her voice quiet and gentle.

I could not speak. Words were piled up in my mind, but my tears would not let the words out of my mouth. I was not ready to admit my loss out loud. How could I say that everyone dear to me was dead? I couldn't, I just couldn't.

"What is that you have in your arms, Nene?" the woman asked me. *Nene* means baby in Guamanian and is used by family to other family members. My heart melted a little in hearing this woman's endearing greeting to me, but I still could not find my voice to respond.

Looking down, I saw that I was still holding my mother's little statue.

"You should carry only what is necessary to live on, little one," the woman continued.

I kept walking and ignored the woman's words. I knew I was disobeying an elder, a serious sin on the island. Nanan Beha had taught me to honor and obey my elders, but not this time. I held tighter to Mary.

"What is your name, Nene?"

I continued to walk and look down. Finally, the woman stopped asking me questions but continued walking by my side. I did not want to talk with her but was glad she was close.

We finally arrived at the caves and filed inside. I found a flat spot, sat down, and leaned my head on the cave wall, the woman close by. The other villagers settled in. For a moment I savored the cave's safety and the silence and fell into a peaceful sleep as I held the Virgin Mary close.

COCONUT PALMS

CHAPTER 5

A Plan

I OPENED MY EYES FROM A DEEP SLEEP. IT WAS DARK. WHERE WAS I? For a few moments I did not remember. Like a powerful wave in the ocean's surf, memories of the previous day's events rushed in. I was still in the dark cave, but I could see light tiptoeing in the cave's entrance. My companion, the woman with the white pearl cross, had stayed nearby and still lay sleeping. I stood up quietly and realized that I was very hungry. I tenderly placed my statue in a nearby hole in the cave and covered her with leaves and branches. Mary would be safe. I moved toward the entrance of the cave.

I had always been an early riser. When I lived with Nanan Beha and Nina Maria, we got up very early and each day I said my prayers of thanks for another day. Then I started my chores. Nanan Beha did not allow me to waste the day lying in bed.

"How are you to know your purpose in life if you just lie in bed?" Nanan Beha would ask. "You must get up and celebrate the day. Give thanks and find your place in the life that has been given to you."

She also insisted that I have a plan for the day. "Each day is a gift," she often said. "What will you do with the gift of another day?"

I always thought of something to do. Some days I did extra tasks around the house. Other days I ran alongside the dirt road that led to the Standard Oil Company tank and picked flowers. Some days I counted the number of birds I saw in one hour. Nanan Beha encouraged me to do whatever felt good. There were no unimportant plans; all plans were good. Plans gave me something to do.

Here in the cave, what plans could I have? I was not sure what to do first, so I followed my instincts and went in search of food. I would find food. I felt so much better now that I had something to do.

When I left the cave, the island's bright colors greeted me. The Japanese had not bombed much near the caves since they posed no threat. The familiar scene calmed and delighted me: bright green banana trees full of yellow fruit; brown and green coconut trees with an abundance of coconuts; and mango trees full of red, orange, and green mangoes. Each leaf of the banana tree had multiple shades of green. I imagined the angels stood in line awaiting God's instructions about how to paint my beautiful island. Where were the angels and God yesterday when nature's canvas had been obliterated? I tried to stop thinking of the bad and center on the good. Nanan Beha said that bad thoughts were like a disease in the mind and that they could smother all the good in the world if I let them.

During this early morning time it was quiet except for the occasional chichirika, egigi, and monarch that flew from tree to tree enjoying the buffet of insects. I had learned from Nanan Beha to always have a respect for all life. I could hear her saying, "There is no one life better than another, including the animals. Just because you walk on two legs and you have a mouth that can get you in trouble does not make you better than God's other creatures. We all have a place in God's world." I could hear her as if she were standing behind me.

"But they cannot pray, Nanan Beha," I would challenge.

"And how do you know that they are not praying, Bernie? Do you understand the language of the bat or the bird or the bee? Just because you cannot understand their language does not make your language better. Be humble and grateful that you are a part of the world. All creatures are a part of this world too." Nanan Beha often told me that everything was equal in God's eyes, including animals and plants.

"Isn't it sad that the Americans kill the animals?"

"Bernie, it is not your place to judge others. Death is a normal part of life. We can never copy God's work in our business of making the animals look alive again, but it is important work to try to copy the beauty of the animal when it was alive."

My stomach growled, reminding me of my task at hand. I snapped back to the present to continue my search for food. I saw a coconut tree and remembered my dear friend Antonio.

"Use your feet like a monkey, Bernie. Watch them and then do what they do," he had said when I told him I didn't know how to climb a tree. "Look. They climb with their feet and hands. See them gripping with the soles of their feet and pulling with their hands?"

The first time I climbed a coconut tree, I forgot I was a girl and pretended to be a monkey. It worked. In less than a minute, I grabbed a coconut, carried it down, and cracked it open. It was the sweetest coconut I had ever tasted.

On this still, quiet morning, while everyone else was asleep, I climbed the coconut tree closest to the cave and shook it until several coconuts fell to the ground. I climbed down, walked over to a mango tree, picked a couple of mangoes, and then pulled several ripe bananas from a nearby banana tree. After finding a rock with a sharp point, I cracked the coconut hard on its seam and turned it just as Nanan Beha had taught me, until I was able to pull the coconut apart into two halves. Immediately I put one of the coconut halves to my mouth to drink the sweet clear coconut water, which was sweeter than I had remembered. I bit into the end of a mango, peeled off the skin with my teeth, and then bit into the soft orange fruit. Nanan Beha liked her mango hard and green—not quite ripe. She would cut the fruit into slices and eat it with salt and pepper. I smiled at the memory of the first time I tried a mango her way, but I still preferred a ripe mango, orange and juicy. After peeling and eating a banana, I was full.

Surrounded by the serenity of nature, I sat quietly. I hung onto the quiet, the freshness of the grass, and the slight breeze scented with the nearby ocean. I noticed other islanders cautiously leaving the cave to get their breakfasts. Several of the men peeked out of the cave before stepping into the light. Others looked up at the sky, searching. It had not occurred to me to be careful. Was there danger here too?

By the time I was seven, it was my responsibility to prepare meals. I knew exactly what to do because of all the hours I had watched Nanan Beha and Nina Maria.

"Do you think you are magically going to know how to cook, Bernie?" asked Nanan Beha. "You must watch and then do as I do."

"But I am too short to reach the stove."

"You are not too short to push that box over there in front of the stove so that you can stand on it and reach, are you, Bernie?"

I understood then that cooking was as much my job as it was anyone's. Every day the first task after morning coffee was to make a big pot of rice. After washing and rinsing several cups of rice and placing it in a large pot with water, I let it cook for about thirty minutes. We used that pot of rice for meals throughout the day. In the morning, we had eggs and rice; at lunch, steamed vegetables and rice; and in the evening, we used the leftover white rice to make fried rice and served it with chicken or fish cooked on the grill.

By age seven, I stopped waiting for other people to cook my food. There were times when Nanan Beha was busy with customers and

Nina Maria was late coming home, so it was my responsibility to make dinner. Everyone was responsible for everyone, but now I was responsible only for myself.

Oh, how I missed having people to cook for and someone to share the early morning with. As I looked at the trees where I had just harvested my breakfast, the branches seemed unusually quiet. At this time of the morning, Nanan Beha and I usually saw the chichirika with its red-brown feathers and the egigi, which sat on tree branches singing beautiful songs and showing off its bright feathers. Usually there were so many birds that I had to cover my ears so I could hear myself think. Perhaps the birds, just like the humans, were scared. Perhaps they were hiding in their own caves.

Suddenly I could not chew and swallow. Had the birds been killed too? The hard memory of loss covered me. I remembered that I was alone and must come up with a plan. Nanan Beha would expect me to figure out what to do next, but I did not know where to start. I had never had to start with nothing.

I started with what I knew—that I had no family, no friends, and no home. That was not good, but almost everyone else was in the same position. I felt better knowing that at least in that way I was not alone. I stood up and started back toward the cave. Most of the islanders were awake now. Several were gathering food.

Among the villagers who had escaped to the caves was an old man whose head was covered with a worn straw hat. His shoulder-length hair was in disarray. He, too, was alone, even though he was surrounded by people.

There was a man and woman with a young girl about four or five. They huddled together as if to form a shield around the three of them. The little girl clasped something tight to her chest. From where I was sitting, the object looked like a doll. Her father tried to break her grip with the object, but she did not let it go. He soon gave up and drew both his daughter and wife to him.

There were several young men sitting in a circle talking earnestly about communicating with other villages, the Japanese landing on the island, and how many people were alive from Sumay. They also were discussing something called the Insular Guard. I did not understand what they said but could tell from their faces that they thought it was all very important.

The woman with the white pearl cross who had befriended me earlier walked toward me. She was taller than most Guamanian women. Her long black and white hair was tied up in a tight bun. She greeted me with her kind face and pleasant smile

"You look rested, Nene."

One of her front teeth was missing. I was oddly comforted by that as I remembered that a kind woman from long ago, Nanan Juna, also had a front tooth missing. I had forgotten her until this moment. It was important to find anything that was a reminder from the past.

"Do you feel like talking to me today, little one?" she asked gently.

"My name is Bernidita, but I am called Bernie."

"How old are you?"

"I am eight years old."

"Who are your people, Bernie?"

I liked when she called me by my name. "My Nanan Beha …" I started to explain but had to stop. A large lump crowded my throat like food that I could not swallow. I knew I had to tell her about losing my family. My heart felt like it would burst. Without warning, the lump in my throat exploded in a flood of tears as I described the events of the day before.

"My Nanan Beha, Nina Maria, they were at the church when it was bombed." I still could not form the words that my family was dead. Somehow I felt that if I did not say the words, I could hold on to the hope that they were still alive.

"Do you have other people, Nene?" The woman gently continued with her questions. I could see in the woman's eyes a mirror of my own pain.

"Nanan Beha has a sister who lived in the village, but I am not sure where she is. She was supposed to be at the church when … when the bombs came. Nina Maria is Nanan Beha's daughter and we all live together in Nanan Beha's house in Sumay. I don't know where Nina is either." I had to stop talking for a few minutes so I could breathe again. My heart, so full of tears that had not yet come, pressed on my lungs, making it hard to breathe.

"We live …" I stopped suddenly to correct myself. " We lived in the two-story house."

"Nanan Beha is … was … a taxidermist. My godmother, Nina Maria, worked in many different places on the island. When the bombs came, Nina Maria was not at home. I think she was at church with Nanan Beha. She sewed clothes and helped with old people around the island when she was not sewing or baking."

"I know of your godmother and your Nanan Beha, Nene. Both do good work. Your Nanan Beha has taken care of many children who had no families. Were there other children in your home besides you?"

"When I moved in, all of the children had moved out. One boy had recently left to join the priesthood and another left to start a taxidermy business in Agana. When the bombs hit, I was the only one at home. I left the church before … before the bombing started."

A steady stream of silent tears covered my cheeks. I tried very hard to stop them, but they just kept coming. And still my heart was filled with sadness.

"We will find your people, Bernie," the woman told me. "You must have faith and pray to our Lord Jesus that we find them soon. Yes?"

"What is your name?" I asked her.

"You can call me 'Grandmother Lilly.' I know that may sound strange to call me that instead of 'Nanan Beha.' My mother was an American military nurse who worked in the TB wing of the hospital in Guam. She married my father, a Guamanian who worked as a maintenance man at the hospital."

I nodded and started to walk back to the cave, leaving Grandmother Lilly walking behind me. I needed to pray. I could do that. I would begin praying right away. I would say a rosary for Nanan Beha and

Nina Maria and all my friends. Saying a rosary for each of them would take me hours, but I could do that. I felt a little better now because I had something to do. I had a plan.

JAPANESE SOLDIERS SURROUNDING AN AMERICAN FLAG

CHAPTER 6

Coping

I LOST TRACK OF HOW MANY DAYS HAD PASSED SINCE THE FIRST bombs dropped and how many nights I had slept in the cave. I was no longer going to school or church and didn't even know what day of the week it was. Soon after we took shelter, the bombing started again. Even though no bombs landed close to our cave, the haunting sound was everywhere all the time—even in my sleep. Was I dreaming the sounds all through the night? I could not tell what was real and what I was imagining. Terrified that danger waited outside the darkness, I did not leave the sanctuary of the cave.

On the island, even if I did not know the islanders by name, there were no strangers. Men were uncles and women aunties. Several of the men took turns leaving the caves to go somewhere. I didn't know where they went, but I was happy when they returned. My two favorites were Uncle Herman and Uncle José. Uncle Herman was fourteen and Uncle José sixteen. Both were about five and a half feet tall, a normal height for a Guamanian man. Both had light brown skin, black, shiny hair, and slanted eyes, characteristics that meant they were probably Saipanese like me. They were always together, talking or playing catch. I thought that they might be brothers and asked if they were.

"Uncle José, are you and Uncle Herman brothers?"

"Brothers? I could never be related to anyone that ugly!" José said, swallowing a laugh.

"Uncle Herman is not ugly. He has a very nice face." I was upset that Uncle José said something bad about Uncle Herman. Uncle Herman just smiled.

"Herman's face is nice? Ha! It's nice if you are a dog!" José started laughing. I could tell that he was not serious.

"So you are not brothers, Uncle José?"

"No, Nene. We are not brothers. Not by blood. But we are brothers in how we feel about our island."

"What does that mean?"

"There are certain people, the Japanese, who are trying to take over our island and we must protect it. We are not officially part of the

Insular Guard, but we are doing what we can to help them. Do you know anything about this group, Nene?" Uncle José asked.

"No, I don't."

"The Insular Guard is a group of Guamanian men who work with the American military to keep our island safe. We are not old enough to be in the Guard but we want to help. There are many of us who think that the Japanese are coming soon and we must help the Americans maintain control so the Japanese do not take over our island." Uncle José was no longer laughing. He was very serious. I watched as he walked away, his head held high.

I turned my gaze to Uncle Herman. I felt as though I knew him but couldn't pinpoint how. I felt at peace around him because it seemed he knew me and cared very deeply for me. The first day I ventured from the caves, I saw him behind me. He was peeling a mango and eating it. His face was round, with wide cheekbones and a large mouth that opened to show his bright white teeth when he smiled. I liked his face and his ready smile. He walked up to me and offered part of his mango.

"No, thank you. I already ate my breakfast. What is your name?"

"My name is Herman. Where is the woman who was with you last night?" Herman seemed protective of me. Of course, that was not unusual on the island. People often watched out for each other.

"I think she is still asleep in the cave, " I said.

"What is her name? Does she have family with her? Is she bothering you?" Herman fired his questions at me, but I did not feel uncomfortable in his presence.

"Her name is Grandmother Lilly. She walked with me from Sumay. My name is Bernie. I don't know if she has family with her. And no, she is not bothering me." I watched Herman as he looked behind him at the group of young men gathering together.

"She calls herself 'Grandmother'?" Herman was confused by the American word for Nanan Beha.

"Grandmother Lilly told me that her mother was an American military nurse and her father was Guamanian. They follow many American customs in her family. I trust her. Please do not worry."

"I have to go now, Bernie. Call me or José if you need anything, okay?"

I nodded and he was gone. I knew the men were planning to leave the caves again. As always, I wondered where they went. The men who left were the young. The older men advised the younger ones to stay in the caves, but the younger men did not listen.

On the days that Uncle Herman and Uncle José were gone, I tried to keep busy. I made a broom from some bush and tree branches and swept around the caves. I helped prepare simple meals without any fire so as not to attract any unwanted attention. Work always helped take my mind off my troubles. Nanan Beha had taught me that work was as important as eating or breathing. One of my chores was to help with the animal waste in the taxidermy process. Nanan Beha removed most of the insides of an animal before preserving it and placed the waste in a box on wheels, which she put by the back door. It was my job to roll the box to the edge of the jungle, empty the waste, and leave it there. One day the lure of the sunshine was so strong that I decided to wait until the evening to move the box. When I returned from play-ing with my friends, an unhappy Nanan Beha greeted me.

"Bernie, you did not move the box this morning."

"You are right, but I will do it now. Why was it important for me to do it this morning? Did it hurt anything to wait?" I could tell by her flat, thin lips that Nanan Beha was showing me more patience than I probably deserved.

"Everyone has a job to do in the world, Bernie. We all depend on each other. I thought the waste was no longer in our back yard."

I still did not understand why this mattered so much. My puzzled look prompted her to continue with the explanation.

"When you empty the animal waste at the edge of the jungle, it allows other animal friends to come from the jungle and help us dis-pose of it. It is important that these animals help us with this task there in the jungle rather than in our back yard. Imagine how surprised I was when I found two boonie dogs enjoying a feast in our back yard!"

Boonie dogs! Now I understood. These were vicious animals that could tear the flesh from a human. Nanan Beha could have been in danger.

"I am sure that they prefer eating their meal near the jungle, where they do not have to face a frightened woman with a wooden club. When you take it to them, they wait until you are gone before they do their job. Because you chose to not do your job, they came looking for what is theirs, and then they had to deal with the pain that comes from being too close to Nanan Beha's home!"

That was the last time I forgot to do this job the right way at the right time. Now without a home or any family, I was responsible for doing what I thought needed to be done. So I came up with a list of daily jobs. Each morning I removed the old "bedding" and brought in fresh grass and leaves for our bedding. Next I gathered fruit for breakfast for me and anyone who wanted to eat with me. Then to keep my mind busy, I talked to people in the cave.

I learned more about Grandmother Lilly, whose given name was Lillian, but I never called her by her first name because that was disrespectful. Grandmother Lilly had lost her daughter and son to the bombings. Everyone who found sanctuary in the caves had lost friends or family members. I never saw Grandmother Lilly cry or heard her talk about her loved ones. I could not understand why.

"Grandmother Lilly, why don't you mourn or cry about losing your children?"

"Is there a reason you think that I do not mourn, Bernie?"

"Well, I never see you crying, and we are together often."

"People mourn differently, Nene. I miss them terribly, but at this time I must give my attention to the living. I am grateful for life, and I know that I will see my daughter and son in heaven one day. My husband died in an accident at work shortly after our daughter was born, and I know I will see him again too."

Grandmother Lilly seemed at peace. I could not figure it out. There were some days when the hurt cut through my heart like a dull knife. Father John, our village priest, had talked about heaven often during Mass. He had described it as a place where there was no suffering, hunger, or violence. Everyone who went there shared their happiness with God. If I knew for sure that I had lost my Nanan Beha and that she was in such a wonderful place, it would have been easier to accept her being gone. But this was still a conversation that I could not have with myself or anyone else. My mind was convinced that Nanan Beha and Nina Maria were gone forever, but my heart was holding on to the hope that they were not.

I tried to be grateful for being spared my life, but it was not easy, especially at night. As I lay next to Grandmother Lilly, I waited until I heard her slow, rhythmic breathing. Then I moved out of my make-shift bed and wandered to the opening of the cave to look at the stars in the night sky. My life with Nanan Beha in Sumay had been so won-derful. I thought that finally God was no longer mad with me, but I now saw that I was wrong. Once again He had taken away everyone that I loved. Why had He left me here alone? What possible reason could He have? Why hadn't I been killed along with Nanan Beha and Nina Maria? Could it be that He was still very angry for whatever horrid deed I had done? But if He was still angry, why had He given me five happy years?

To stop my mind from racing at night, I would leave the cave, even though Grandmother Lilly and Uncle Herman told me I was forbid-den to leave it at night. I left anyway because I had to see the sky. If I could see the stars that Nanan Beha and I had shared on so many eve-nings after we had finished our chores, then perhaps I wouldn't feel so lonely. For at least an hour each night, we had sat quietly together watching the stars. Although neither of us said a word, I felt closest to Nanan Beha during these times.

Here was the same sky, the sky we had happily shared so many times. But this night when I looked up at the sky, I was filled with sadness. All my resolve and discipline not to mourn was gone during these times. I missed Nanan Beha and Nina Maria so much. I tried not to cry, for fear I would wake the sleeping villagers. As I sat on the hard ground, I pulled my knees to my chest and laid my head on my knees. I finally just closed my eyes and let my tears come.

In the midst of my crying, I felt a soothing hand on my back slowly moving back and forth. I stopped crying but did not look up. My face was hot with embarrassment. I had awakened one of the villagers. The hand stopped moving but stayed on my shoulder. Nanan Beha used to rub my back to comfort me. We both remained still. After a few moments I felt fine, like everything was going to be all right. I turned to look up and thank the gentle soul who had come to me, but no one was there. I was alone but not alone. How could this be?

Could it be that Grandmother Lilly had similar experiences? Is that why she could bear her loss? At that moment I felt that all would be well. I got up from the cold ground and returned to my place in the cave.

In the morning I needed this newfound reassurance more than ever. The young men who had left the day before, Uncle Herman and Uncle José among them, returned to the cave, their faces tired and full of fear. I moved closer to them so I could hear the conversation.

"The Japanese have landed on the island and the Americans are no longer in charge. The Japanese are killing the American soldiers instead of taking them as prisoners. Some of the Americans have escaped into the jungle. The Japanese are gathering the Guamanian survivors on the island to place them in camps. They know we have escaped to the caves and are coming for us. Soon the Japanese soldiers will find all of us," Uncle José explained to the entire group. "Members of the Insular Guard have been captured and killed for aiding the Americans. We can do nothing but wait," José continued.

Some villagers prayed, others cried. I remained still and calm, enveloped in an unfamiliar, reassuring peace.

Uncle Herman came to me about an hour later and asked me to sit down so we could talk.

"As you heard José say, the Japanese are coming, Nene. It is important that you do exactly as I tell you. First, do not look into their eyes!" he said fervently. "If you do, they will see you as disrespectful and hurt you."

I had always been taught to be respectful of my elders, but this was different.

"Do not say anything to them. Most of the Japanese soldiers do not know our language, so they will not expect anyone to respond to them," he continued.

He put his hands on my shoulders and looked deep into my eyes. "Do you understand what I am saying to you, Bernie?" I saw how terrified he was and nodded.

"I understand. I will not look at their eyes and I will not say anything.

I will look only at the ground when the Japanese come."

"I will be translating for the Japanese soldiers if they let me. There are not many Guamanian who speak Japanese. I learned long ago from a childhood friend how to speak Japanese. It is important that the Japanese do not know that you and I are friends, so I will not speak openly to you. I am doing this to protect you. Do you understand?"

I nodded. Only then did he drop his hands and slowly walk away. In the weeks between the first day of the bombing and the day the Japanese captured the islanders, Herman and I had formed a strong bond. Each time I felt lonely or needed to talk with someone, he was nearby. He made me laugh and forget my troubles. I felt safer when Uncle Herman was close by.

That very evening we were captured. Five Japanese soldiers came equipped with bayonets and whips. Most of us were still in the cave when we heard shouts coming from outside the cave. Uncle Herman knew what they were saying.

"They are ordering us to leave the cave," Uncle Herman translated. "If we don't leave on our own, they will come into the cave shooting. They say that if we leave quietly and in an orderly fashion, no one will get hurt," he continued.

Then his voiced changed. He was no longer translating. "There are many more of us than there are of them, but we have no weapons. It would be suicide to resist. The Imperial Japanese Army is expert in using the bayonet. We need to do what we can to stay alive. We must walk out slowly in one line and put our hands up. Look down at the ground and do not have eye contact. I will go first."

Uncle Herman and Uncle José's experiences with the Insular Guard and the American military saved lives that day. Uncle Herman led us out of the cave in a single file. No one looked up. No one spoke. The Japanese soldiers spread out on either side of the island people as we began the long ten-mile walk away from the caves to a camp in the city of Manenggon, where thousands of other islanders would join us. We were told that the camp would be surrounded by barbed wire fences lined at the top with large circles of razor wire. It seemed we could only count on one thing these days: life had changed—and not for the better.

VIRGIN MARY

CHAPTER 7

Manenggon

THE WALK TO MANENGGON, A VILLAGE ON THE SOUTHEASTERN side of Guam, was long and sad. The soldiers were cruel. They prodded us with their bayonet blades as though we were cattle. Everything around us had been destroyed. Huts were still burning. All the vegetation along the road was charred from the recent fires. People, some still alive, were lying all along the road. We were not allowed to stop for any reason except to quickly relieve our bladders. I saw many wandering children. Guamanians had always taken care of their children, but now there were many of us without parents.

I thought about Nanan Beha and how she felt about unwanted or abandoned children. Before I arrived in Sumay, as many as ten children had lived with Nanan Beha. She had a special place in her heart for children and said that every child deserved a good start and felt it was her purpose in life to give them one. I remembered that one time she came to the rescue of a special little boy who came to one of her grand parties that involved hours of preparation. The night before the party she marinated several whole chickens in a soy sauce and vinegar marinade. Before dawn she began grilling a huge hog on her grill outside and at midmorning she started grilling the chicken.

As the meat cooked, Nanan Beha prepared other Guamanian treats in the kitchen, including *finadene*, a pickled condiment made of chopped onions and hot chili peppers mixed in soy sauce and lemon juice. The night before she made a variety of desserts, including my two favorites, *ahu* and *kalamai* (sweet corn pudding made with coconut milk and sugar). She also made a fresh fruit salad with mangos, bananas, coconut, and watermelon. Then she stored it our icebox, one of the few in our little village.

By midafternoon, her friends, relatives, and customers began to arrive. Nanan Beha's brother-in-law brought his cousins, who took charge of the music. Soon everyone was laughing, singing, dancing, and enjoying the Guamanian feast. My favorite part of the parties was the dancing. Nanan Beha said I could dance as long as music was playing. She was right. My friends and I danced the Guamanian Cha-Cha for hours.

One of her customers, Jeff, an American soldier, brought his seven-year-old son, Michael, to one of the first parties I attended. Michael's mother, also American, had died of complications from a Portuguese Man o' War sting just months before the party. Jeff, who had no family on the island, was having a rough time coping with her death and raising Michael alone. Jeff turned to alcohol to help him cope. To make matters worse, Nanan Beha heard that Jeff had received orders for an isolated tour, which meant that he could not take Michael with him. Jeff was supposed to leave in two weeks.

As the party continued into the late evening hours, Nanan Beha watched Michael with his father. Jeff kept drinking and became increasingly abusive toward his son. At one point Jeff raised his voice and ordered, "Get me another beer, boy."

"Daddy, please don't drink more. Mommy would not want you to drink so much," Michael pleaded.

"Don't tell me what your mother would want. When I tell you to do something, you do it!" Jeff stood up to yell in Michael's face and lost his footing. When he fell to the ground, he hit his head hard on a large rock and landed face down on the ground. Several of the soldiers ran to Jeff's aid. One placed his thumb on Jeff's wrist to feel his pulse.

"He is unconscious. His pulse is weak. He needs medical care," yelled a fellow soldier, who quickly carried Jeff to a car to drive him to the hospital.

Nanan Beha, walking toward the crying child, said to the driver, "I will take care of Michael. Please let me know as soon as you can what the doctor says about Jeff."

Then she turned her attention to the frightened little boy. "Michael, do you remember me? My name is Nanan Beha. Your father needs to have a doctor look at his head where he hit it. It will be a long time before we hear anything about how he is. You will stay with me and Bernie in my home. Come and let me wipe your tears."

With a cool cloth, she gently wiped the tears from Michael's face and held him close. A short time later he stopped crying. When the party was over, she tucked him into the bottom bunk in the boys' bedroom on the second floor, where many other little boys had found safety and love. My room was on the ground floor. Nanan Beha had converted a storage room into a bedroom for me.

The next day Nanan Beha received news that Jeff had died in the night from a brain hemorrhage. In six months Michael had lost both his parents. Nanan Beha delivered the news to Michael about his father's death.

"Michael, I must tell you some news about your father. When he fell last night and hit his head on that rock, the fall damaged his brain. He is no longer on earth. He went to be with your mother in heaven."

"I don't understand. My mommy is dead. How did my daddy go to visit her? Does that mean my daddy is dead too? I don't want my daddy to be dead too. I don't want Daddy to go with Mommy. I miss my mommy." Michael started crying, gasping for air in between sobs.

Nanan Beha held him until he stopped crying. The poor boy was exhausted. She knew she had her work cut out for her because Michael did not know that there is a place we go after death. She taught every-one in her care that there is a circle of life: everything and everyone are connected.

"Michael, even though your mommy and daddy are not here with you, they are still in your heart. They are just in a different place and you will see them again. Nothing ever ends. You can't see them right now, but you still feel them in your heart and in places and things around you," she explained.

"But I don't want to wait for them. I want to be with them now," Michael sobbed.

"Let's go for a walk and see what we can find," Nanan Beha said as she took his hand in hers. Mittens, our cat, had given birth to a litter of kittens two weeks before. We were keeping her and her kittens in a box under the back porch.

"Look what we have here, Michael. Mittens has some new kittens." Soon Michael was lost in the love of soft meows and kitten fur. Nanan Beha always knew what to do to make things better.

In the next few months Nanan Beha gave special attention to Michael to help him deal with the loss of his mother and father. He was respon-sible for feeding all of them and making sure they had water. He was also responsible for making sure they had lots of love.

Several months later, Michael could finally talk about both his par-ents without crying. It was not long before there was a young couple looking for a boy to adopt. Nanan Beha would miss Michael's gentle manner, but her home was a temporary refuge for most of the little ones who passed through. Nanan Beha made sure that Michael had his favorite kitten when he left. He smiled and hugged her neck. During the children's time with her, she was their guardian angel.

Nanan Beha was also a tough taskmaster. Expectations were clear at her house. I had to go to school and church and do my homework. I also needed to help cook the meals, clean the house, and wash the clothes. The children who had stayed with Nanan Beha in the past didn't do household chores; their work was in the back of the house with the taxidermy business. After leaving Nanan Beha, several of them started their own taxidermy businesses; others, well versed in what it takes to run a business, branched out and opened up other types of shops.

One of my best memories of Nanan Beha was listening to her stories. After dusk, on days when she was in the mood, she turned off the lights in the living room and lit a candle. As the dim light flickered, she told stories about the Taotaomona, the spirits of the first people of the island that fought against those who wanted to hurt it. Nina Maria also told stories; her stories were about my mother. These were my favorite.

A cry took me away from my thoughts. I looked around and discovered that a soldier was kicking a woman twenty feet ahead of me over and over again. Soon she was silent—and dead.

Like us islanders, the Japanese were small people. But their bayonets, uniforms, loud voices, and angry faces made them more powerful. What I had just witnessed made that clear.

I could not believe what I saw along the walk to Manenggon. A ten-year-old girl was carrying a toddler on her back and holding hands with a little boy and a little girl. I figured that the brave, exhausted girl was now an orphan doing the best she could to take care of her siblings.

There was talk about a woman who had given birth during the walk. Immediately after the baby was born, the Japanese soldier gestured for the new mother to stand. The Japanese soldier stabbed the baby through her heart with his bayonet and forced the mother to leave the baby on the side of the road. What kind of people were these soldiers?

I witnessed one of them yelling at another mother in Japanese, pointing his hands forward, moving his arms up and down like a bird. From the way he was moving, I thought he was trying to tell the woman to walk faster. The woman likely thought the same but first bent down to pick up her two-year-old child. Infuriated by the delay, the soldier thrust his bayonet through the woman's leg. As she started to fall, I took the toddler from her. But she did not fall. She stood up as if nothing had happened and continued to walk, looking straight ahead, her face blank. The Japanese soldier, satisfied that the woman was not going to hold up the crowd, turned away to look for more troublesome islanders.

I continued to hold the child on my hip as we all walked forward, but I could not help staring at the woman. She did not look at me and somehow continued to walk. A few minutes later, a man walked between me and the woman and whispered something to her. She nodded and said in Guamanian that she was not in pain.

He then turned to me, reached for the baby and said, "Thank you for helping my sister. I will take my nephew now." He walked close to his sister in case she needed to lean on him. The woman continued to watch the soldiers, somehow knowing that any sign of weakness would end her life.

I heard some of the adults saying that Manenggon was to be our new home. Once we arrived we would build a camp that would be our home. We learned that the camp would be surrounded by a barbed wire fence, which we would also construct. We would be locked inside the camp. There was some excitement because we were to be placed at the northeast end of the Manenggon River, where we would have fresh water, unlike other islanders who would be held in camps farther down the river. I had heard there were camps on other parts of the island as well, but I did not know where.

As we walked, most of us kept our heads bowed. No one spoke when a soldier was nearby. No one laughed. I had travelled this road once before on an oxcart with Nanan Beha for a festival to celebrate Santa Marian Kamelen, the saint of Manenggon. Dozens of people had joined us. We sang, laughed, and ate the whole way. Who would recognize those same people today?

Everything we owned we carried on our backs—a change of clothes, whatever medicine we had left, and a couple of handfuls of food. Toys, utensils, tools, furniture, and keepsakes were all gone. They had either been destroyed by the bombs or left behind in the cave.

Only Grandmother Lilly knew that I had saved and still carried my precious statue of the Virgin Mary. I wrapped Mary in an old piece of cloth that Grandmother Lilly gave to me and tied it to my back with some rope from Uncle Herman. Uncle José gave me one of his shirts. Grandmother Lilly told me it was very important that I continue to look like one of the boys. With my short haircut and the loose shirt on my tiny frame, I definitely looked like a boy. I did not know why it was so important that I look like a boy, but I did not care. What was important to me was that I had salvaged my only possession when we left the caves.

After we arrived, we were not allowed to rest. We immediately started constructing the eight-foot-high metal fence. I could not believe that our people could do so much work, as tired as we were. To keep from cutting their hands, the men who put the razor wire in place had to wrap their hands with palm leaves that they first tore into strips and wrapped around their pointer and middle fingers and palms of their hands. The razor wire on top added another two feet to the top of the fence. There were so many of us, about a thousand, and we were herded inside the fence like animals. When I heard the metal lock on the chain clink against the metal fence, I stood back from the fence and hid behind one of the few coconut trees so the Japanese could not see me. For the next half hour I stood still and watched the Japanese soldiers through the fence as they walked back and forth with their rifles with bayonets resting on their shoulders, ready to kill.

In Sumay for the past three years I had felt totally secure and loved living with Nanan Beha and Nina Maria, but in my heart, because of all the times I had moved as a child, I didn't feel any place was permanent. Now, fenced in this crowded camp and watched like an animal,

I felt that this place was despairingly permanent. I felt like I was going to be here in this camp for a long, long time.

CHURCH IN SUMAY, 1941

CHAPTER 8

Hair

O UR FIRST NIGHT AT THE CAMP, WE WERE FORCED TO LIE ON THE damp ground, huddled together like a pack of dogs. As I lay there, I prayed that the misery would stop and that somehow I would wake up and discover it was all a bad dream. But when I woke the next day, the misery continued.

The soldiers separated us into groups. People who could not walk or use their hands or arms were placed outside the camp. In disgust, one soldier spit on a man who limped and whose face was disfigured.

The Japanese were taking people who were different—the crippled, the disfigured, and the physically and mentally challenged.

Nanan Beha had taught me to value all life. People who were different were not supposed to be discarded. All life had value. Nina Maria had told me that people who were different were special spirits sent by God. I remembered Julie, who came to live with Nanan Beha a week after my sixth birthday. Julie was born with a crooked back and could not walk. Her parents and other family members tried to take care of her physical needs. They made sure she was fed, bathed, and dressed. They exercised her limbs every day. They gave her everything she needed physically. Even so, her health declined. Julie was seven years old when her mother and father brought her to Nanan Beha's house.

"We cannot give her what she needs. Although she is alive, her spirit is dead. There is no light in her eyes." Julie's parents had done what they could, but it was not enough. They prayed that Nanan Beha could help.

For a week, Nanan Beha did not leave Julie's side. She ate with her, slept with her, and told her stories. She talked with her about the history of the island. She held her close and told her how loved she was and how special she was in God's eyes. In only two weeks Julie changed. She smiled often and her eyes danced. Nanan Beha would wheel Julie out to the porch so that she could talk with her while she worked on her taxidermy projects. After a month, Julie's parents returned to Nanan Beha's house and were amazed at the difference in their little girl. They took Julie home with them but brought her back every month to spend a weekend with Nanan Beha.

After one of Julie's visits, I talked with Nanan Beha about what Julie's parents had said. "They called you Julie's angel on earth, Nanan Beha. Are you an angel from heaven?"

"We are all here to love each other without judgment, Bernie. Remember that."

And I did. I tried to love everyone, but I could not love the soldiers. The soldiers did not love the island people. Here they were on our beautiful island, sorting us as though some of us were rotten vegetables. They took people every day, and now the soldiers were pulling babies and toddlers from their parents' arms and taking them to the soldiers who were located outside the fence. What was to happen to the babies? Why were they being taken?

"Grandmother Lilly, where are they taking the babies?"

"I don't know, Nene."

Mothers, fathers, aunties, and uncles pressed their faces against the inside of the fence. As we gathered against it, one of the Japanese soldiers shouted to the group.

"わなければならない." (Watch what happens. You must obey.)

He kept shouting and flailing his arms.

"あなたが従わなければならない, あなたが従わなければならない." (You must obey. You must follow.)

Suddenly Uncle Herman stepped forward. Uncle Herman turned to all of us and said, "I understand their language. I will try to find out why they are taking our children."

He walked over to a soldier and addressed him in Japanese. The soldier was surprised, but without looking at Uncle Herman, he responded. They continued talking for a few minutes, and then Uncle Herman came back to us and said, "The Japanese soldiers want us to watch what they are about to do. They are telling us that we must obey them. The one in charge is their general, General Takahashi."

Uncle Herman turned to the Japanese general, carefully listened to his words, and then translated the terrible news. "The general told me that our loved ones would not be returned to us."

Several islanders ran to the fence and started shaking the fence in protest. In response, one of the soldiers outside the fence fired at their feet. There was nothing we could do to stop them. The soldiers gestured with their guns for everyone to back away from the fence. The babies and old people were placed in carts and hauled down a dirt road. We were trapped inside the fence while our loved ones were taken from us.

Later that night, Uncle Herman came to Grandmother Lilly and told her about his conversation with the Japanese general. They thought I was asleep, but I heard the whole conversation.

"The general told me he wanted to kill our people in front of us to show us what would happen if we did not obey them." Uncle Herman confided. "I needed to do something, so I told him that our people must not watch the deaths take place and that I understood what they were going to do." He stopped talking, took a few long breaths, and continued. "I told him the island people would revolt and that they would not stand by and watch their babies and old ones be murdered in front of them and do nothing. Then I assured him that if they did not witness the massacre, they would be hopeful that the ones taken would survive. I told him if he continued with his plan, there would be no strong bodies to work rice fields."

I turned so that I could see Grandmother Lilly's and Uncle Herman's faces. Uncle Herman's face looked tired and worn. He continued, "Though I could not save the lives of our babies and their grandparents, I tried to keep those who remained inside from seeing the horror that was about to happen and prevent their deaths, so I told the general I understood that he must eliminate the weak and work the strong. I assured him I would translate his orders and tell the islanders that they must obey. The general followed my wishes but said, 'These savages are not important. They will be killed.'"

Uncle Herman held his breath again, just as he must have done while waiting for the general to consider his suggestion. He continued, "A few minutes later, the general ordered the other soldiers to take the 'nonessentials' away from the camp to kill them. Grandmother Lilly, this was the hardest thing I have ever had to do. Although I know I saved many from dying, I still feel like I failed."

I had not known that Uncle Herman and Grandmother Lilly were so close, but I was not surprised. Grandmother Lilly had a way about her that invited closeness.

Uncle Herman continued to talk. "I breathed a sigh of relief that our people would not have to witness the inevitable. I also knew that I had to tell those who remained that their loved ones would not be returning." He paused. Tears slipped from his eyes and he quickly wiped them away.

I did not realize until then that I had been crying silent tears too. We honored and respected our old people, and our babies were the hope of the future. But these awful soldiers did not hesitate to take them from us and snuff out their lives like they snuffed out their cigarette butts.

Grandmother Lilly put her hand on Uncle Herman's shoulder. "You are so brave and wise for a man so young. You did the right thing, Herman. During this terrible time you will need to trust your instincts, as you did today. This will not be the last time you will need your courage."

Uncle Herman sat quietly with Grandmother Lilly. I don't know how long he stayed because I fell asleep. I did not want to hear any more about the camp. I wanted to escape into my dreams.

The next morning I was awakened by a woman screaming hysterically. The cruelty was continuing. I sat up and saw a soldier slap the woman in the face to quiet her screams. "My daughter ... where is my daughter?" The woman had been searching for her daughter, who was expecting her first child. She had looked around and realized with horror that her daughter and the other pregnant women were gone. In the night the Japanese had taken them away too.

Uncle Herman walked toward me and Grandmother Lilly to explain what was going to happen that morning. The Japanese were deathly afraid of disease, and in order to protect themselves, they were going to vaccinate us. But it was not to be like getting a vaccine from the travelling school nurse. The efficiency of the Japanese was also brutal.

"When they yell, quickly step into a line," he told me.

Once in line, Grandmother Lilly whispered in my ear, "At the end of this line is a soldier who is giving us shots. When you walk through the line, you will hold up your arm so that the soldier can give you a shot. He is using a gun-shaped tool but it has needles, not bullets. You must not cry out when the needles pierce your skin. You must be strong. Do not look at the gun and do not look at the needles. Do you understand, Bernie?"

"Yes, Grandmother Lilly, I understand." I walked up to the soldier when it was my turn and everything that Grandmother Lilly described happened. When I was in front of the soldier, he used this gun-shaped tool to shoot a circle of needles nine times into the fleshy part of my upper left arm. The whole thing was over in less than a minute. I actually moved past the soldier before I felt the pain. By then, Grandmother Lilly had received her shots. She grabbed and pulled me away to keep me from crying out. I looked at the open sores where the needles had torn through my skin and bit my hand to keep from crying out. I knew that my skin, once healed, would scar—a sickening memento of this terrible time. Many people fell ill and died from the vicious vaccinations. Their immune systems were too weak to deal with their infected open wounds.

In the following days the soldiers continued to sort us into groups. Two categories were left. Men, boys, and married women were needed to work in the rice fields. Single women and girls as young as seven were needed to "service" the Japanese soldiers in the Japanese "comfort house," which was located outside the camp. A few people didn't fit into either category, such as two young men who were mentally handicapped but were able to take orders. We later learned they were assigned to take care of the oxen as well as cook and clean for the soldiers.

Two soldiers put all the boys in one line and all the girls, except me, in another. When the soldier got to me, he gestured for me to stand in line with the boys. I looked at Grandmother Lilly. She just said, "Do what you are told." She had no emotion on her face. At first I thought the soldier had made a mistake, but I moved into the boys' line.

There were twin girls placed in the girls' line right after I was put in the boys' line. Their parents, Juan and Rose, were watching like all the rest of the family members. After the boys and girls were separated, the two soldiers pushed the boys back toward their families and then started walking in the opposite direction with the girls.

Juan stepped forward, demanding that his girls be released. Without hesitation, one of the soldiers slammed the butt of his rifle across Juan's head, knocking him to the ground. Rose cried out and went rushing to him, kneeling on the ground with his head on her lap. She called out his name and began whispering into his ear, "Please don't die. Please don't die." The soldier grabbed her by the chin and turned her head to the left and then to the right as if he was examining her.

"私たちは快適な家に彼女を使用することができます。" (We could use her in the comfort house.)

The other soldier grabbed the first soldier's arm.

"夫は死んでないまで。" (Not until the husband is dead.)

The first soldier released his hold of Rose's face. Juan remained unconscious. Those of us who remained cried and held onto each other. I was confused. I took Grandmother Lilly's outstretched hand to walk back to our hut. I turned one more time to see the girls all being led away with the soldiers. One of the twin girls was already crying.

Once we were alone, I asked Grandmother Lilly about what had happened that day.

"Why did that soldier grab the woman's face, Grandmother Lilly?"

"He was looking at her to see if she would be someone to put into the comfort house, Nene.'"

"Why didn't the soldier take her with them?"

"The soldiers were letting wives stay with their husbands. It was good that her husband was still alive. Otherwise, she would have been lost to the comfort house."

"Is the comfort house a bad place? Why was I put in line with the boys, Grandmother Lilly? Where did the soldiers take the girls? Why was everyone crying?" I was very sad but didn't know why.

Grandmother Lilly took a deep breath. Her bright eyes looked clouded and tired. She looked like she had been crying too.

"Bernie, first let me tell you that you were put in line with the boys because the soldiers think you are a boy. It is very important that they keep thinking that about you."

"Grandmother Lilly, I don't understand. Why do they think I am a boy and why it is important that they think that I am?"

"Bernie, I am going to tell you something that may be hard to understand. When you cut your hair on your birthday three months ago, it changed your destiny."

She continued, "Before the Japanese started sorting our people for jobs they could do, Herman told me that girls were being separated from boys so that they could be taken to the comfort house and that boys would be working the rice fields."

"What is the comfort house, Grandmother Lilly?"

"It is a place where the soldiers go when they are no longer working." She hesitated before continuing, "The soldiers will use the girls however they want to use them. Some of the girls will do household chores for them. Some will wash their feet and hair, and some will be made to do things no child should do with a man. If the girls refuse to do what they are told, they will be beaten until they obey. It is not likely that any of the girls taken to the comfort house will be released for as long as the war lasts.

"That is why, Bernie, it is important that we keep your hair short. The soldiers know that girls on the island only have long hair. So we must continue to keep your hair short."

The Japanese allowed married couples to stay together as long as there were no babies. Brothers and sisters, cousins and friends paired up to pose as married couples to avoid the horrible fate of single young women. Most who went to the comfort house never saw their families again; they were either killed or died of starvation.

Sitting in the hut late that night, I thought about the girls being taken away from their parents. Now I was more grateful than ever for the way that Nanan Beha had punished me for cutting my hair.

Her words echoed in my head: "You will get on your knees at the celebration of the birth of our Lord on Christmas Day with your shame. We will keep your head shaved until after Christmas. Maybe then you will learn your lesson." She had saved me from what could only be a horrible fate. After all, no island girl had short hair. Even the Japanese knew that.

A USAAF B-25B BOMBER ON ITS WAY
TO ATTACK TARGETS IN JAPAN

CHAPTER 9

Work

WORKING THE RICE FIELDS WAS HARD. EVERY DAY, FROM EARLY morning before the sun rose until evening when darkness crawled over the island, we worked the fields. Some workers planted rice, some used machetes to cut the reeds, and some thrashed the rice from the dried rice reeds. From the time we arrived until we left, my job was to reach down under the water and pull the reeds of rice from the waterlogged soil. We did not take a break unless the soldier who guarded us wandered away. It would be a certain and horrible death if we were caught resting, so we were always on guard.

My work was monotonous—bend at the waist, push my hand into the mud at the root of the rice reed, grab the root, pull up, stand, place the reed in the crook of my arm, and start again. The only way to escape the drudgery of the rice fields was to daydream.

Even unpleasant memories were a relief. Nanan Beha began teaching me the taxidermy trade after my seventh birthday. I disliked working with dead animals. Cleaning their insides was very messy. The worst part was how sad I felt seeing an animal without the glory of life. I remember working on a bat and thinking that he had once spread its wings to a span of twelve inches, his eyes had gleamed looking for insects, his fur had stood up after spotting a meal. Without life, the bat was limp and empty. We would do what we could to restore it to its original beauty, but whatever we did would be a poor substitution for God's work.

A loud voice from behind me snatched me from my daydream. The Japanese soldier assigned to our work crew cracked his home-made whip on the ground. He held its bamboo handle in his right hand and flicked his wrist to make the thin leather strand cut through the air. Each day this soldier targeted one of us. I was determined not to be today's target, so I was very careful not to let the soldier see me watching him.

Every day I did what I needed to do to blend in. My close friends, mostly boys, gave me their discarded shirts and pants. We were allowed to bathe only once or twice a month. Not everyone knew my secret. Only the islanders who had huts close to where Grandmother Lilly and I stayed knew that I was a girl.

The screams and cries from the house each night were torture for all of us, but were the worst for the parents of the little girls. Grandmother Lilly had told me that the girls would be doing things that no child should do with a man. Whatever that was, it was hurting them. Whatever it was, it was terrifying them. And whatever it was, their hopeless and anguished cries tore at our hearts. At first Juan resented me because I had escaped the horror that his daughters were enduring, but it was not long before he changed and helped me keep my secret. Each week he shaved my head with the machete used in the rice fields, and each week I thanked him. Once, after an especially hot day in the fields, Juan stood motionless for a moment and then took me into his arms and held me while he cried. I did not pull away. I had never seen a man cry before the war, but in the camp I saw it happen all the time.

A cracking whip pulled me back again to the rice field. The soldier noticed that I was not working as fast as the others and cracked his whip in front of me. I put my head down, dropped my shoulders, and continued working, trying to blend in with the dirty water and reeds in the rice field. It was not a good thing that he had noticed me daydreaming

I watched the soldier from the corner of my eye. He was new to our group. Although they all were vicious and brutal, this new one seemed to hate us more than the others. He watched each one of us very carefully. At one point, this new soldier stood behind one of the older islanders, waiting for the old man to make a mistake. He was watching the old man like one of the jungle brown snakes watching an unsuspecting mouse. He wanted to hurt him. However, he did not get his chance because the old man continued to work and the soldier didn't have a reason to hurt him.

Earlier that week I had asked Uncle Herman why the Japanese hated us so much.

"The Japanese soldiers are not just doing their job. They hate us. They look at us like we are worse than the brown snakes that crawl on the island. Why?"

Uncle Herman explained, "Bernie, to the Japanese we are the enemy because we are a protectorate of the United States. To them we are not people. And even if we were, the soldiers are simply doing what their leaders expect them to do.

"I don't understand how someone can love to kill, especially for no reason," I continued.

"War is a terrible time. People on both sides do things they would normally not even consider doing. Soldiers receive orders to commit horrible acts and obey without question. They don't like being here and know that if they killed us all, they could go home. But doing that would ruin Japan's reputation. The world does not care that we are being held in camps with little food and water, but I think there would be an uproar if people on the mainland knew the Japanese were murdering us en masse for no reason."

"But Uncle Herman, they *are* murdering us for no reason. They have already killed all the babies and pregnant women from my village. How could anyone want to cause so much pain? The soldier who watches us at the rice fields is so vicious."

"You must be talking about Corporal Kikuchi." Uncle Herman said.

I never thought about the soldiers having names. "You know his name, Uncle Herman?"

"I don't know all their names, just a couple. But I do know his name. He has made it a personal mission to kill Americans and those allied with Americans."

"Why? What would make someone want to kill?" I could not understand it. Before the war, I found it hard to kill a bug. Even though I helped Nanan Beha with the taxidermy business and worked around dead animals all the time, I had not killed any of them.

"People always do things for a reason, Bernie. Corporal Kikuchi has his reasons."

"What kind of reason would make it acceptable to want to kill, Uncle Herman?"

"Earlier this year the Americans conducted an air raid. Japan probably thought they were invincible and that no one could get to them, but these Americans did."

"What does that have to do with Corporal Kikuchi?" Uncle Herman continued.

"Before Corporal Kikuchi was stationed in Guam, he was not a soldier. He was a fisherman. When the Americans bombed part of

Japan, several civilians died, including Corporal Kikuchi's wife and five-year-old son."

"How do you know about this, Uncle Herman?"

"When I am around the soldiers, they forget I am there and often talk openly. I overheard a conversation between Corporal Kikuchi and one of the other soldiers."

"War is awful, no matter which side you're on, isn't it?" I said. I never thought it was possible, but for a moment I felt sorry for the soldier.

"Corporal Kikuchi held his son in his arms when he took his last breath. He was thankful that his son had died, since he had lost both his legs in the bombing. There was nothing left of his wife."

Uncle Herman was staring at the ground, and we were both quiet. Then he continued with his story.

"Corporal Kikuchi told the other soldier that when his family died, he died too. He left his life as a fisherman and joined the Japanese Imperial Army. As he sees it, his mission is to take the life of every American that he can. He has become one of the best soldiers both with a whip and with a bayonet."

"Uncle Herman, a terrible thing happened to his family, but he still should not want to kill more."

For the first time, Grandmother Lilly, who was standing nearby, spoke. "I know it's not right, Nene. Sometimes it is not important whether someone is right or wrong. Sometimes it is more important to understand why people do what they do. Now you understand why Corporal Kikuchi is the way he is."

I was not sure why, but I felt different about Corporal Kikuchi.

Grandmother Lilly went on. "He may think killing gives him satisfaction, but I think it is only fueling his hate more. Even if he were able to kill every American he met, it would not bring back his wife and son. And in the end, he will still be filled with hate. His real enemy is hate, not the Americans."

After this conversation I was more grateful to be alive and to feel love for Uncle Herman and Grandmother Lilly. I also did not mind the work as much. Yes, it was backbreaking and tedious, but it saved me from dwelling on the camp's horrid conditions and left me so tired that each night I lay on the hard ground, I immediately fell asleep.

That night I dreamed about something that had actually happened. One day Nanan Beha had overheard me making fun of Antonio because of the work he did for a local pig farmer feeding pigs and cleaning their pens.

"You smell just like the pigs' pen," I told Antonio, laughing at him. Antonio walked away with his chin on his chest.

"So you think Antonio's work is not valuable, Bernie?" Nanan Beha said to me once Antonio was out of sight.

"He just cleans the messes the pigs make, Nanan Beha. How valuable can that be?"

"How many others stand in line to do Antonio's work, Bernie? Do you see others waiting to work like Antonio does?"

"No, Nanan Beha. There is no one else who wants to do that work."

"Bernie, if no one cleaned the pens, the pigs would stand in the filth all day. Then what would we be eating when we eat the pig? You enjoy your bacon at breakfast and your ham in the tomato stew, don't you?"

I had never thought about what would happen if Antonio did not do his work.

"All work has value. You would do well to remember that."

When I woke the next day, I thought about what Nanan Beha had said about work. Even if the Japanese did not admit it, we were valuable to them. They needed the rice we grew and harvested. Some of it fed the soldiers and some was taken away on their ships. I decided to believe that what I was doing was valuable work.

Some of the older men had difficulty just getting up in the morning. I was young, so my bones and muscles did not tire as easily. I was grateful for my youth and grateful for work; it had saved my life. I chose to believe that my work mattered and that my life mattered.

JAPANESE MILITARY OFFICERS PREPARE TO EXECUTE
THREE CHAMORRO MEN, 1944.

CHAPTER 10

Execution

THE GUAMANIAN PEOPLE HAD ALWAYS BEEN A PEACEFUL PEOPLE—
forgiving each other easily and accepting newcomers. Hundreds
of years before, the Spanish nearly killed all the Guamanian people
when they tried to convert what they saw as a "heathen" culture to
Christianity. They did this by intimidating and threatening the island
men and then killing them when they did not do what was expected.
The Spaniards did not understand how much the Guamanian women
influenced the island's culture. In the Guamanian tradition, older

married women were powerful. They exercised control over family life, property, and inheritance. Their status was reflected in rituals, legends, and ceremonial events.

The traditions and beliefs of the Guamanian people were all but forgotten with the arrival of the Japanese. We changed after the Japanese threw us into the concentration camps, raped our women and children, killed our babies, and beat up our old people. More and more of the islanders, especially the younger men, started to discover their rebellious spirits. Their angry faces and clenched fists revealed their resentment. One day I watched as a soldier snapped his whip at Uncle José's feet. Uncle José stared back at him with no fear. He looked the soldier directly in the eyes and refused to look down. The soldier repaid José's arrogance with three slices of his whip across Uncle José's back, but he showed no pain. I was holding my breath the entire time, afraid that the soldier would kill him, but he didn't—not then.

Soon after I arrived at the camp, I overheard conversations that some of the young Guamanian men were spying for the Americans. I was so afraid for them—and for good reason. Uncle Herman told me many times that the Japanese soldiers were loyal to their cause and heartless when it came to their captives, especially ones who chose to disobey. They forbade anyone from trying to contact Americans who had escaped and were still alive on the island. Several Americans had fled the Marine barracks and were not caught by the Japanese soldiers. The soldiers were ready to demonstrate that they were serious about their rules.

One overcast day I learned how serious. Other than the dark sky, the day was like all the other days: work, heat, work, bugs, work, hunger, and the eventual arrival of night with its escape to my dreams, which took me to places where no Japanese soldiers existed.

But on this day something felt different. Though we had settled into our usual routine, I detected some tension. I noticed Uncle Herman and the other young men stealing whispers. A Japanese soldier was signaling us to return to the bus to take us back to camp. Some left the rice fields and walked toward the dilapidated American military bus that took us to and from the rice fields each day.

Although I welcomed the opportunity to leave the drudgery early, I did not like the sick feeling rising in the pit of my stomach. When we arrived back at the camp, everyone started to walk toward the center of the camp. Several soldiers were motioning us to move toward the center of camp. I wondered why they were going that way. We did not usually gather in the middle of the camp unless the soldiers ordered us to. As if being pulled by a magnet, I left the bus and started walking toward camp. Then I saw Uncle Herman hiding behind a big banana tree inside the camp and gesturing urgently for me to come to him.

He was looking down at the ground and then looked up as if he were searching the heavens.

"What is wrong, Uncle Herman?"

He looked at me with apprehension and resignation. "Bernie, you know that many of our villagers are trying to help the Americans, yes?" his voice cracked.

"Yes, I know." I knew that some of the villagers including him and Uncle José were trying to help, but I did not know how.

"I'm sure you know that José has been a strong leader."

I nodded yes and waited as Uncle Herman took a long, deep breath.

His voice quivered as he said, "The Japanese now know about José." He stopped talking, swallowed hard, and continued, his voice soft at first, as though it was an effort to speak. "José is going to be killed today. That is why all the villagers are going to the center of the camp. I have only few minutes to talk about what is about to happen, Bernie."

He knelt down on one knee so he could be face to face with me. "I am going to translate for the Japanese when they are ready." He held my face in his hands and continued. "Bernie, it is very important that you listen to me now." Angry tears filled his eyes. "The Japanese are going to tell everyone that they must watch as José is killed. If anyone turns away, they will also be executed."

He stopped for a moment and then continued. "I am telling you what they are about to do because you must know so that you do not cry out. You must be prepared for what is going to happen and not turn away or show any emotion. If you do, Bernie, you also will be killed. Do you understand what I am telling you?" he asked, gripping my arms.

"Yes, I understand you, Uncle Herman," I answered. But I did not and could not understand. Uncle José was going to be killed today, in front of everyone? He was going to die? Uncle José was like a brother to me. In spite of all the difficulties of living in the camp, he always had a playful spirit. Several times he walked around bending his knees, swinging his arms, and brushing his hands on the ground in his hilarious imitation of a monkey. He was always trying to make me laugh. I could hardly believe what Uncle Herman was telling me.

Herman continued to describe in detail what was about to happen when the soldiers executed José and two other male villagers. All three had been helping the Americans who got away from the Japanese.

"The Japanese are going to use their swords to cut off the men's heads. Then they will cut off their arms and legs and put all their parts in the graves that they have made the three men dig.

"I hate this war. I hate the Japanese. I hate that I have to tell you this. I hate that you have to see what you are about to see."

For a moment, Uncle Herman looked like a small boy, scared and confused.

"Bernie, there will be blood. José will die quickly and he will not be in pain, but there will be a lot of blood. Some villagers will not be able to keep from crying out, so there will be more executions. What is about to happen will be horrible and terrible and much, much worse than I have told you," he said, trying to explain the unexplainable.

"When the executions happen, you must look but not see. I cannot tell you how to do that, but you must. I will be standing next to the Japanese soldiers behind José. You must look at the execution but instead see me. See anything instead of the execution, but you must look. Do you understand, Bernie? Do you understand me?"

I nodded. Uncle Herman took a deep breath. He stood up to leave.

"Wait a few minutes until I am ahead of you and then follow me to the center of the camp." He walked away, his shoulders stooped and head hung low.

I counted to ten and then I walked on trembling legs to the center of the camp. Uncle José and two other men were kneeling on the ground with their hands tied behind their backs. They were looking down, facing the open graves that they had dug themselves just minutes before. Uncle José held his chin to his chest and looked down. I could not see his face.

Then I heard Uncle Herman translating the screaming soldiers' ugly words. "I have been ordered to translate a message from the soldiers. They have told me to translate word for word. Here is their message. 'We do not tolerate disobedience. These men have violated our rules. They have tried to communicate with the Americans, and because of these violations, they must die.'"

The Japanese soldier standing closest to Uncle Herman took his sword from his side, slowly raised it, held it up, and then swiftly and effortlessly dropped the blade. I did not move my head. I watched the sword glisten in the sunlight and, in what seemed like slow motion, I watched the blade slice through the air and then, as if through butter, it sliced through Uncle José's neck.

There was a gush of bright red blood. I was fixated on the terrible picture: the sword, the reflection of the sun's light off the blade, the blade slicing through José's neck, and then the color red—red, red, and more red. I watched the execution as Uncle Herman had told me to. I looked and tried not to see. I looked and then I saw past the scene to a tree in the distance. A blood-red egigi sat on a branch behind and between the soldier and my dear friend Uncle José. I stared at the bird with its bright red feathers.

In the next moment, the soldier cut off Uncle José's arms and legs. The red bird opened its bright red wings and stood completely still. I wondered why it did not fly away. I looked away from the bird for a moment and saw the soldiers stack Uncle José's lifeless limbs and head onto the trunk of his body. Two of the island people were ordered to lower his dead body into the open grave. I looked back on the tree in the distance. The red bird was still there.

I did not turn away. I remembered what I must do. I did not cry. I did not cry. I did not cry. I looked directly at the scene and saw nothing. Nothing. Nothing except the blood- red bird. I looked around me. I could see that people were screaming in terror as more islanders were killed, but I could not hear them. I saw the red bird close its wings and then open its wings, but it didn't fly away. Everything else was a blur—a bad, bad dream. The soldiers slashed their swords through the air and through arms and bodies and necks. Uncle Herman had been right. What I had just seen was much, much worse than what he had described. I stood completely still. I would not move, I could not move. It was just me and the bird with its crimson red feathers flapping.

In that moment, something happened to me. Part of me tried to maintain focus on the beauty of the island in the distance, far from the execution site, but I could not forget watching my friend die. I wanted to see only the red color of the bird and not the red of the blood of my dear, dear friend. I wanted to forget how easily the Japanese soldier had snuffed out Uncle José's life, but I could not. Still, I did not move. I did not cry out. I did not turn my eyes. In the midst of all that had just happened, I had lost my friend and changed. For the first time in my young life, I felt a deep, severe hatred with a heart that was not mine.

*GUAMANIANS AT THE MANENGGON CONCENTATION CAMP
USED THE YLIG RIVER AS THEIR WATER SOURCE. HERE
WOMEN WASH CLOTHES WHILE THEIR CHILDREN PLAY.*

CHAPTER 11

———

Daily Life

AFTER UNCLE JOSÉ'S EXECUTION, I FELT NOTHING. I JUST WENT through the motions of daily life. Each morning the soldiers were at the gate, rattling the steel fence as they unlocked the lock to gather us together to bow to their god. As always, the Japanese priest started speaking in Japanese. He didn't look at us. And, as always, the soldiers stood quietly with their heads bowed. We stood still and all faced the same direction. There were no statues or altars—just air. Then we bowed our heads so that our chins touched our chests. In this way, we showed our respect for their god. Each day they watched us to make sure we kept our heads down and our mouths shut. If we did not meet their expectations, we were whipped, shot, or stabbed. I saw many people die during these worship sessions. I had no idea what the priest was saying or who we were bowing to. I didn't want to worship any other god but had no choice. The only thing I wanted from this part of the day was for it to be over.

Before the war, we were a hardworking, happy people. Working was not something we resented. It was a part of us and showed everyone our individual contribution to the whole of life. We enjoyed our work and we enjoyed our fun. We had parties for everything—baby showers before and after a baby was born and parties celebrating anyone's accomplishments at church or school such as communion and graduation. Of course, marriages, anniversaries, and birthdays were all causes for celebrations. We got together for almost anything with food, music, and most of the time, laughter—even wakes and funerals. Before the Japanese soldiers arrived, we came and went as we pleased. We invited strangers to our celebrations and family meals. We opened our homes to those who were without shelter. But now everything was different. Now we were caged like animals. All of our movements were watched, and if any of our actions violated the rules of our captors, we were beaten or killed.

When we first arrived at Manenggon, we set up life within the confines of our camp according to the requirements of our captors: our three-walled roofed huts had to face the empty space in the middle of the camp so that the Japanese soldiers could see into our living spaces. After we built the huts, we dug holes close to the fence line for our outhouses. When heavy rains or storms destroyed our homes, we rebuilt them with the help of Uncle Herman and the other men. Each storm made rebuilding harder because the coconut trees were dying from too much leaf harvesting.

Soon after we had arrived at Manenggon, Grandmother Lilly and I met Carlos, an old man who had lost everyone in his family including his eight-year-old granddaughter. Grandmother Lilly invited him to share a hut with us. "Grandmother Lilly, is Uncle Carlos your friend?"

"He is my friend now, Nene. Why do you ask?"

"I just wondered why you are letting him stay with us in our hut."

"Carlos and I had a chance to talk during the walk. Before the Japanese came to the island, he had had a rough life. He is an alcoholic and has given up drinking. He loved his granddaughter very much and when she asked him to give up drinking for her, he stopped. His family was his whole life, and he lost everyone. I knew that we could help him heal. Was I right, Nene?"

"Yes, Grandmother Lilly, we can help him."

On our first laundry day, I returned from the river and found Grandmother Lilly saying her rosary and giving thanks for the location of our camp.

"Grandmother Lilly, why are you thanking God that we live in this camp?"

"Because it is in the northeast end of the river. If we must be imprisoned, this location is the best place to be. We are at the top of the river where the water is the freshest," she said with a grateful smile. "We need to be careful with what God has given us. We have enough water for drinking, bathing, and washing. I never forget to thank God for what we have." Grandmother Lilly always remembered to give thanks no matter what. I left the hut to let Grandmother Lilly finish her rosary.

I found it hard to be grateful about our water situation. The Japanese, in an effort to conserve water, limited each person to one bath each month and one laundry day every other week. Although the women continued to wear clothes, it was not long before our clothes were so saturated with the smell of human waste, perspiration, and soil that it was easier for some of the men to shed their clothes and wear only a loincloth to cover their private parts. Of course, I continued to wear short pants and a ragged t-shirt.

Water was not the only staple that was scarce. When we first arrived in the camp, we saw many banana, mango, breadfruit, star fruit, and coconut trees, but with so many to feed, it was not long before they were depleted. As many islanders shed their clothes, I saw the effects of hunger—many of our people were just skin and bones. Even if there had been a surplus of fruit and water, we could not have stored anything for future use because the soldiers did not allow us to have more food than we could prepare for one meal. We were allotted only twenty minutes to eat, not enough time to adequately cook just the handfuls of rice we stole or "found." How strange to harvest rice all day every day but not be allowed to cook it properly and eat our fill. Eating insufficiently cooked rice resulted in bloated bellies for those of us fortunate enough to have food in our stomachs at all.

I was one of the few who had a regular food source. Soon after our arrival at the camp, Uncle Herman asked me to follow him to a hollowed out log near the fence at the rear of the camp.

"Bernie, each day I want you to make sure that you check this place. Who knows, you might find some rice here," he said with a twinkle in his eye.

Each day I went to that place and almost always found rice. Sometimes there was an entire cup—enough for me, Grandmother Lilly, and several others in neighboring huts.

It was my job to clean the eating utensils after our evening meal. I used sandy soil, which provided the needed abrasive material to scrub the food and other residue from our eating and cooking utensils. I wiped off as much of the dirt as I could before quickly rinsing the utensils in the river. We were not allowed to take time to wash our eating utensils, but we could quickly rinse them. It was important to preserve our water supply, so I was careful not to use much water to rinse the sand and dirt from our plates and cooking pot. We were thankful that the river was inside the fenced area of the camp. The top section of the river located at the north end of the camp was segregated for drinking water, and the next section, located midway in the camp, was to be used for cleaning our eating utensils. The third section of the river located at the south end was for bathing and the last was for washing clothes.

We were afraid we would run out of water as we had run out of fruit. But what we feared more than anything was disease. We were particularly vulnerable to tuberculosis because we were half-starved and our ability to ward off diseases was compromised. One evening after dinner Grandmother Lilly and I heard crying coming from a hut behind ours. Esther and her three little boys lived there. Esther was crying and moaning. A man posing as her husband also lived with them but slept outside the hut every night. She was difficult to understand, but it sounded like she was praying for her child not to die. Grandmother Lilly left our hut and went to hers.

She was gone for several hours and looked very tired when she returned.

"What is wrong, Grandmother Lilly?"

"Bernie, Esther is sick and one of her little boys has been coughing for the past two weeks. The little one has been losing weight and refuses to eat. He has had a fever for a week and today he has been coughing up blood." Grandmother Lilly looked at the ground as she was describing the little boy's condition.

"Can a doctor be called to help her?" I asked.

"I am convinced, as is Esther, that she and her little boy have tuberculosis. Her other two boys are also showing signs of the disease. I have heard that although the hospital on the island was destroyed during the bombing, the tuberculosis wing survived. But I doubt that the Japanese will allow this family to receive any medical attention, even though anyone with tuberculosis is a threat to the rest of the camp.

If the Japanese find out this family is carrying the disease, they will likely kill the family and everyone who has had contact with them."

We had dealt with tuberculosis on the island before the Japanese, so I did not understand what was wrong but knew it must be very bad because Grandmother Lilly was so sad. The following evening I found out how desperate the situation had become. After dinner I took our dishes and pot to the river and Grandmother Lilly left for Esther's hut.

"I am going to check on the sick child, Bernie. If you return before me, do not be concerned if I am not here."

Down by the river I took my time washing the dishes. When I arrived back at the hut, Grandmother Lilly had already returned. She was holding her rosary and had her eyes closed. Soft tears were rolling from her eyes.

"Grandmother Lilly, why are you crying?"

"Give me a moment, Bernie. I want to finish my rosary."

This was unusual. Grandmother Lilly usually said her rosary in the morning, not in the evening—and I had already heard her say her rosary three times. After about an hour, she finished saying it a fourth time before she finally put her beads under her makeshift mattress on the ground.

"Bernie, Esther is dead. She stole a knife, cut the wrists of each of her children, and then cut her own wrists. When I arrived in her hut, she was still alive. Before she died, she told me that she could not risk having more of our people killed because of the illness her family carried. She wrapped each of her children so that whoever buried them would not have to look at the face of each innocent child. She asked me to pray that she be forgiven so that she could join her children in heaven. Tonight I said a rosary for this brave woman and her three children. As you know, in our religion, suicide is a sin, so I had to act quickly. I hope I acted soon enough to save them all from Purgatory. Several of the young men kept watch while we buried the young family."

"Why would she kill her three children?"

"Bernie, these are unusual times. No one knows what to do or what is expected of them. This brave woman gave her life and the lives of her children so that our lives would not be taken. The Japanese fear an epidemic. They would have killed us all if they thought she had contaminated us. She will be with our Lord, and He will welcome her to heaven. Neither she nor her children will ever hurt again."

I knew that Grandmother Lilly was right. All of us were trying to find our way during this horrible time. Keeping busy was one way to manage. Learning the soldiers' habits was another. The Japanese soldier assigned to our crew got the crew started in the rice field, walked back and forth for a while along the edge of the rice field, and then left for half an hour. During his absence, most people rested in the shade of the nearby coconut trees, but I used this time to stuff rice into the hem of my pants. I could carry nearly a cup from the rice fields to camp this way. I shared the rice with whomever I trusted not to tell that I was violating a rule. I learned that people did strange things when they were hungry and not everyone could be trusted. One of the other workers who had smuggled rice from the fields was betrayed by one of the islanders. The starving man, angry that he had not been given any of the stolen rice, reported the theft to the soldiers, who forced everyone to watch as they whipped both men, betrayed and betrayer, until they were dead. Uncle Herman translated the message from the soldiers who accused both men of stealing rice that was not theirs.

The soldiers did not bother those who stayed busy and rested less. When we returned to camp from the fields each day, I stayed as busy as I could. I was exhausted, but if I cooked and cleaned in my little hut, none of the soldiers harassed me. I slowly swept in and around the hut at the beginning and end of each day. After meals, I cleaned up the area slowly, tended to Grandmother Lilly and Uncle Carlos, and then finally lay down to sleep.

This was my daily life. Oh how I yearned for the carefree days, but I knew I had no choice but to accept my life as it was now. I did but continued to bring rice from the fields back to camp as often as I could. I was not afraid of being betrayed and caught. After all, I knew that the soldiers paid little attention to an obedient little *boy* who did exactly as *he* was told to do.

A CHILD PEERS OUT OF A MAKESHIFT
SHELTER AT THE MANENGGON CAMP.

CHAPTER 12

Bernie's People

ALTHOUGH SOME OF THE CHILDREN IN THE CAMP HAD LOST PARents, they were not on their own. The Guamanian culture did not allow children to be alone. There were no orphans. Every child had a family and every family was allowed to live in a coconut-leaf hut. I soon learned all about the four families who lived in the huts close to ours.

Joe and Carrie Ann, who were brother and sister, posed as husband and wife and took in twin eight-year-old boys Joey and Brian, who had lost their parents on the day of the bombing. On that day, as the family was walking home from the Feast of the Immaculate Conception, pieces of shrapnel hit both their mother and father, killing them instantly. Both boys witnessed their parents' deaths. Joey had not spoken since, but Brian could not stop talking. Carrie Ann said Brian, who was very protective of his twin, was talking for both of them. Joe and Carrie Ann were devoted to their new charges.

Next to them lived an older married couple, John and Marie, who had lost their three children and eight grandchildren. Marie had been sick and could not attend the feast at the church; John had stayed home to care for her. All their family had been at the church and had perished. They were in their sixties and were healthy but said little to anyone, including each other. They did only what they had to. I think they were waiting to die.

Matthew, Joanne, and their six-year-old little girl, Besenta, lived just across from us. They looked afraid all the time. It seemed they thought they had outsmarted Death but feared their time to be snatched away was imminent. Matthew didn't work in the rice fields. His job was to keep the soldiers' bayonet blades and swords sharpened. Joanne supervised the cooking for them. Besenta was allowed to help in the soldiers' kitchen.

I watched another married couple, Juan and Rose, the couple who had lost their nine-year-old twin daughters to the comfort house. The parents' faces looked ghostly. Rose was not even thirty years old but looked twice that age. Juan spoke with no one except me and

Grandmother Lilly. His face was always etched with rage.

Grandmother Lilly visited their hut as often as she could, trying to be of whatever help she could. One evening she noticed a change for the worse in Juan.

"Juan, are you sleeping better?"

"No, Grandmother Lilly. I have hardly slept since the first bomb dropped."

"Juan, you must go inside your heart to start the healing process."

"How can I heal when my two baby girls are in that terrible place? I can't find peace as long as they are there."

"Rose needs you too, Juan."

"I love Rose, Grandmother Lilly. But she is safe and my girls are not. Every night, when I hear the cries from the comfort house, it tears at my heart because I'm sitting here safe and they are not. I cannot forgive. I cannot heal. My love for them is of no use if I cannot help them. What value is my life with those soldiers, those animals, putting their hands on my babies?"

Though fueled with vengeance, Juan knew he was helpless. If he tried to rescue his young girls, the whole family would be killed. One evening the cries seemed more desperate. I was sitting outside our hut. Grandmother Lilly had just returned from Rose and Juan's hut, where Rose lay sleeping and Juan was as agitated as ever.

I noticed a Japanese soldier exiting the comfort house and saw Juan walking toward the locked gate at the entrance to the camp. Alarmed that a prisoner was leaving his hut, the soldier stood at the door and stared at Juan. Amused at Juan's brazenness, the soldier smiled and then broke into a loud, mocking laugh. Juan snapped. All the anger and rage he had held inside finally reached its breaking point. He started climbing the fence. I jumped to my feet. Where was he going? Didn't he know his fate on the other side of the fence? Grandmother Lilly came out of our hut. We all screamed for Juan to stop, but he continued to climb the fence and reached the top, which was lined with razor wire. His hands and arms dripping with blood, Juan climbed down the other side of the fence. When his feet touched the ground, he walked toward the front door of the comfort house.

The Japanese soldier was no longer laughing. He ran back into the comfort house, which was outside the fence, and raced out with a rifle. The soldier was in a panic. Juan's face was painted with fierce determination, his eyes burning into the soldier, his fists clenched at his sides. The soldier was momentarily paralyzed. After a few seconds, the soldier fired his weapon in Juan's direction. The bullet missed. Juan started running toward his assailant, who shot again. This time the bullet hit Juan in the stomach. Somehow empowered by the injury, he ran toward the soldier, who shot Juan again and again. Each time the bullets hit their target—the unstoppable father.

Juan finally reached the soldier and wrestled the weapon from him. Juan raised the butt of the gun and hit hard across the right cheek of the soldier and then across the left cheek and then over and over again on the soldier's head. All the commotion brought other soldiers, who aimed at Juan from behind. Juan dropped to the ground but not before

Juan's target, the Japanese soldier who had taunted him, also dropped to the ground. Both lay dead outside the entrance to the comfort house.

Juan was dead. I could not believe what I had just witnessed. He was gone. Now Rose had no husband. She would wake the next morning to find she had now lost her whole family. Grandmother Lilly, standing behind me, took me by my shoulders and led me back to the inside of our hut.

"Why did Juan do what he did? Didn't he know that he would be killed?"

"People do things in war that they wouldn't normally do, Nene. Juan let his anger take over his life. We can only pray for his soul and continue to help the living."

"Grandmother Lilly, what will Rose do now? She has no family left now."

"We will find her a husband before tomorrow." Grandmother Lilly knew that the Japanese soldiers would put the unattached Rose in the comfort house if they noticed she was alone.

At the time of the bombing, I had Nanan Beha, Nina Maria, along with Nanan Beha's sisters and cousins. They were my family. Now they were all gone. I could not understand why Juan would give up the only family he had left. I would do anything to have my family again. I reminded myself that I was surrounded by people who had lost family members—some to the bombing, others to our merciless captors, others to starvation and disease.

Initially I was stalked by grief but soon learned how dangerous such a companion was. I could not afford to be distracted by my daydreams, my nostalgia, my emptiness. Not paying attention to what the soldiers wanted every minute was to risk a quick and horrible death. On one occasion, Ricardo, one of Uncle Herman's friends, slipped into a daydream and did not snap out of it quickly enough to satisfy Corporal Kikuchi, who was trying to get his attention. Corporal Kikuchi, probably thinking the young man was ignoring him, killed Ricardo before he knew what had happened.

Having a family was an important part of survival during the war. A family unit, which communicated stability to the Japanese, was not a threat to the soldiers, because family members took care of each other and did not risk inciting the wrath of the soldiers. They did what they were told.

The morning after Juan's death, Grandmother Lilly broke the news to Rose. She also found Luke, a young single man who had been sleeping in the open area, to pose as Rose's husband. The Japanese paid little attention to details and did not notice that it was her husband who had killed one of their own. Life continued in the camp.

Like Rose, nearly all of us had to welcome strangers into our lives. Grandmother Lilly, once a stranger, was now my dear companion. I also cared deeply for Uncle Herman. These two were my people now, my family. But after losing Uncle José, I closed my heart to everyone else as securely as the Japanese closed and locked the gate to the camp each night.

MANY GUAMANIANS SUFFERED FROM MALNUTRITION
DURING THE JAPANESEE OCCUPATION.

CHAPTER 13

Starvation

THE CAMP AT MANENGGON WAS NOT THE ONLY CONCENTRATION camp on the island. Uncle Herman told me that Guamanians were herded into similar camps throughout the island. He said they all had barbed wire fences lined with circles of razor wire. These fences not only kept us inside the camp, they also kept us away from food. Although there were parts of the island with an abundance of food from nature's buffet, we were restricted to the little food that was inside the fence.

Before the war, food was everywhere. Fruit trees were as plentiful as flowers on the island. On Saturdays, after I finished helping Nanan Beha, my friends and I ran to the edge of the jungle and to the caves to play. I loved to climb trees and run around in search of adventure. One Saturday I met my friend Nellie near our favorite cave. Nellie was very fragile and fearful. She told me that I was the bravest person in the world because I wasn't afraid of anything—climbing trees, catching snakes and beetles, running through the jungle, and even stuffing dead animals. I was also brave enough to go into the caves alone. I didn't think anything I did was brave—I was just curious. One Saturday Nellie and I sat outside our favorite cave, eating bananas, mangoes, and coconuts. Unlike other girls my age, I climbed the coconut tree to retrieve the luscious fruit instead of waiting for someone to get it for me.

"Nellie, today let's explore a cave."

"But, Bernie, we can't! What about the Taotaomona? My brothers tell me these spirits of our ancestors wake when they hear children playing. If we wake them, they will be angry and take us away from our families."

"We will be very quiet, Nellie. Even if we wake them, I want to see one of them and ask what it was like to be on the island so many years ago."

"You want to talk with the Taotaomona, Bernie? But we can't. They will hurt us. They will be angry with us. We just can't."

Nellie started to cry and shake. Tears gathered in her coconut half. The thought of talking with the spirits was too much for her.

"Don't cry, Nellie. We won't go into the cave. And we won't look for the Taotaomona. It is too pretty outside anyway to spend time in a dark cave. We will have a different adventure. Let's go to the beach and find treasure!"

We jumped up, leaving our lunch on the ground, and ran to the beach. I wondered where Nellie was now. I hoped she was still alive. I could almost taste the banana, see the orange mango flesh, and taste the sweet coconut water on my lips. At that time, I had never even thought about the food I wasted. Now I would give anything to have the leftovers I had run away from. I promised myself I would never waste food again.

We knew there was plenty of food on the island to feed everyone, including our captors, but they would not allow us out of the camps and were too afraid to explore the unfamiliar jungle terrain. There was plenty for them to be afraid of—snakes and poisonous lizards as well as the Guamanians and Americans on the loose, and of course, the Taotaomona. Besides, why would the Japanese penetrate the unknown? They were not starving. They had plenty of canned food from their mother country and were free to fish. They had no reason to be worried about food. If we starved to death, they didn't care.

I wondered whether the world knew that our island had been captured and that we were starving. I figured that they did not know, because if they did, they would help. All of us—children, parents, uncles, aunts, cousins, brothers, sisters, and grandparents—were growing weaker each day. Even so, the Japanese still expected us to work in the rice fields fourteen to sixteen hours a day.

We were not just starving from a lack of food. Our spirits were also starving. Was it just a year or two ago that these same people wore chubby cheeks and wide smiles? We had become aliens with bleary-eyed expressions, absent of any joy. We used to be an energetic, fun-loving people, but now we mechanically went about our daily activities.

After working fields, eating my evening meal with Grandmother Lilly and Uncle Carlos, and cleaning up, I found a place to sit and watch life in the camp. The single older men and women sat on the ground near their huts—not talking or moving, in order to preserve their strength. Some couples talked with other couples, but most did not socialize. There was too much risk in trying to get to know someone only to lose them to the rage of the Japanese soldiers.

Almost every evening the young men met and talked. They took turns meeting at different huts before returning to their own spaces. One evening I asked Uncle Herman what the men talked about.

"Uncle Herman, isn't it dangerous for the young men to meet every evening?" The Japanese had told them they could not meet, but they did it anyway. I noticed that the longer the islanders did without food, the more risks the young men were willing to take.

"Bernie, we have to do something. It is hard for a man to stand around and not try to make a difference. We talk about anything we have heard from the soldiers or visitors to the camp. We share any communication that we can. We have to do this to have hope."

"These meetings are important, aren't they Uncle Herman?"

"Yes, Nene. They are important. Everything we see might be useful to others on the island. Information is as important as food to us and to the Americans," Uncle Herman explained.

"But, who do you share information with? And how? You are inside this fence like everyone else."

"Bernie, I cannot tell you details about how we communicate, but I can tell you that Americans are on our island, and I, like many others from camps throughout the island, give them information. We tell them everything that happens."

"Will more Americans come back, Uncle Herman?"

"They will be back, Bernie. You can be sure of that."

I was very proud of him and the other young men who were putting their lives in danger for the good of all of us. At the same time I was afraid for their lives.

"I still can't believe you are fifteen. You are so smart and you are a good leader. Are you sure that you will not be discovered having these meetings, Uncle Herman? I do not know what I would do if I lost you, too, to the soldiers."

"Do not worry, Nene. We have a very good system in the camp. Ever since we lost José, we have been extra careful. If the soldiers come, we will know soon enough to stop the meeting and return to our huts. "

These meetings were just as important to the young men as the handfuls of rice they stole from the rice fields. Information was scarce, as was food, which was getting increasingly scarce each day. Soon the stolen rice was the only food available. People took horrible risks to feed themselves. The only islanders small enough to fit through the razor wire were the smallest of the boys. One by one, they climbed the chain-link fence to take their turn trying to get through the circles of razor wire. One by one, they failed and fell. Many of them died from the wounds they incurred trying to escape the camp to find food and bring it back to camp.

Family and friends could not ask for medical assistance when the boys were injured. The Japanese would not be lenient, and the Guamanians faced certain risk of losing their child to the executioner's sword for trying to flee. Instead, adults dared to hope that their children would survive, but only the strongest children survived the wounds from the rusted razor wire.

From the beginning of our stay in the camp, Uncle Herman brought me, Grandmother Lilly, and Uncle Carlos rice from the general's camp. He had stopped leaving the rice in the hollowed out log because someone had discovered our hiding place and was taking the stolen rice. He started bringing rice to me every couple of days. I tried not to think about my hunger. Instead, I imagined a world where there was plenty of food. When I worked, hunger cut my insides and my stomach cramped. I retreated to my daydreams, where I had plenty of mangoes, coconuts, rice, eggs, and chicken.

After a day's work, when my hunger pains were the worst, I pictured myself sitting down with Nanan Beha and Nina Maria at our kitchen table. I could smell the food and took plenty of time to remember the details of how the food looked and tasted. I pictured Nina Maria making my favorite dish of fried rice with lots of onions and peas and carrots. I could smell the onions frying in the oil with the rice and imagined Nina Maria adding the soy sauce. At the end of the day, Nina Maria had often made a double batch of fried rice with the left-over white rice for the next day's lunch. Sometimes I felt like I could actually taste each morsel.

Each night as I lay down to sleep, my hunger pulled at my stomach. With pictures of plates full of delicious food playing over and over in my mind, I repeated my personal vow each night: "I will survive this horrible time and when I do, I will always have food for my friends and family." I knew I would survive; I also knew that I would keep my promise. As I repeated my promise over and over again, I kept the growing hunger monster at bay.

GUAMANIANS WORKING IN A RICE PADDY FIELD WITH
JAPANESE MILITARY PERSONNEL MONITORING

CHAPTER 14

Determination

THE JAPANESE SOLDIERS TOOK EVERY OPPORTUNITY TO HARASS us. It was as if they wanted us to fight back so they could justify beating us. If one of us moved too fast to try to please the soldiers, that person would find himself on the wet ground being beaten with the butt of a soldier's weapon. When commanded to get up and work, if we moved too slowly, more beatings came. We were at the mercy of the mood of each individual soldier.

Before the war I knew what was expected of me. Nanan Beha made it clear what she wanted me to do, and as long as I did as I was told, my life was uncomplicated. The same was true at school and church. I loved my teachers and I think they loved me too. I was curious about everything. Although my grades were average, my teachers commented often on how diligent I was and how much they enjoyed having me in class. I did struggle though with my numbers and tried extra hard in math class because I adored my teacher, twenty-four-year-old Miss Salas, who was the smartest woman I had ever known—besides Nanan Beha and Nina Maria, of course. She always answered my questions and was very patient with me. I think she knew that I was trying as hard as I could.

After class one Friday afternoon Miss Salas told me she was going to visit Nanan Beha and Nina Maria. When she saw my concerned face, she told me not to worry and handed me an envelope. "Bernie, please give this to Nanan Beha. It's a request that I be able to visit with her next Friday."

Nanan Beha was surprised when I handed her the note.

"Did you disobey your teacher, Bernie?" Nanan Beha asked.

"No, Nanan Beha. I don't think so," I said hesitantly. After all, sometimes my curiosity and playful spirit got the better of me. One day I was helping Miss Salas clean up after class. I saw notes about our science assignment for the next day on her desk. She was going to show us how two ingredients we used at home could cause an explosion. When she stepped out of the room, I read the instructions and could see that the ingredients and equipment were right there. I couldn't resist. According to her instructions, I poured the baking soda and vinegar into a glass jar, which had a piece of aluminum foil in it. When I heard her coming back to the room, I quickly lay the lid on the jar. Just as she entered the room, the contents of the jar exploded out of the top. What a mess it made! I was so relieved that Miss Salas appreciated my curiosity and did not send a note home to Nanan Beha and Nina Maria.

When Nanan Beha asked me if I had disobeyed Miss Salas, I thought I might be in trouble. Trying to reassure both of us, I said, "Miss Salas would have told me right away if I had been disobedient, Nanan Beha. She is very honest about how she feels about all of her students."

"It sounds to me as if Miss Salas has to say a lot about your behavior, Bernie. Is this true?"

I was getting very nervous and unsure about the reason for Miss Salas' visit. Then suddenly I remembered what she had told me when she had handed me the note earlier that day: "Bernie, you are not in any trouble. I just want to have a talk with your family about how you are doing in school. There is nothing to worry about. I visit the families of all my first graders."

Relieved that her words had come to mind, I blurted them out verbatim. Then Nanan Beha looked even more confused.

"I have never had a teacher visit me unless there was something wrong. Well, we will find out soon enough the purpose for the visit."

Later in the evening, when Nina Maria arrived home from work, she came to my room to talk with me about Miss Salas's note and the upcoming visit.

"Bernie, please do not worry about Miss Salas's visit on Friday. I have heard very good things about your teacher. She is known in your school as a teacher who cares very much about her students. I am sure she has your best interests at heart."

I loved talking with Nina Maria. I always felt good when we talked. In all the time we had been together, I never remembered her being upset about anything.

On the following Friday after school, Miss Salas arrived right on time for her meeting. Nanan Beha sent me to the village store and told me not to come back for one hour. She let me wear her gold watch with a diamond on the face right on the number "12". Nanan Beha had taught me how to tell time, and I loved it when she told me to make sure I came back after one hour. I looked at the watch before I started for the store. It was 3 o'clock. When I returned at exactly 4 o'clock, my teacher was gone. Nanan Beha and Nina Maria told me all about the visit.

Nina Maria began, "First of all, Bernie, you are not in any trouble. Miss Salas likes to visit all her students' families so she can get to know them. Miss Salas was very respectful to me and to Nanan Beha."

"Miss Salas is independent, smart, and resourceful. I like her. She told us that you are a good student—always attentive and punctual. She also told us that you do your homework every day," Nanan Beha said.

"We were eager to find out if we could do anything to help you with your studies, Bernie," Nina Maria added. "She said that you try very hard on your numbers, and she thinks you could benefit from extra help after school. I know you are very curious and sometimes it is hard for you to slow down and concentrate. She explained that you do not have trouble paying attention in reading or writing class."

Nina Maria had taught me how to read soon after my arrival in Sumay, so when I started first grade, I was the only one in my class who could already read—but I wasn't ahead in math.

"Miss Salas has a plan about how to help you. She wants you to stay after school for an extra hour each day. During this time she'll give you extra homework and tutor you. She thinks that soon you will be as good with your numbers as you are with your reading. So beginning on Monday, you will spend an extra hour at school," Nanan Beha explained.

I was so excited. "Nanan Beha, I promise I will do good, and after I have done my homework, I will do my chores." I could not wait to get started.

"Bernie, until Miss Salas is satisfied that you are doing well enough with your numbers, you do not have to work in the taxidermy shop. Do your chores around the house but there's no need to work in the shop. She believes that with this extra time after school and the additional homework, you will be at the head of your class with numbers too," Nanan Beha declared.

I could not believe my good fortune. Although I never complained, I did not look forward to working in the shop.

"Let's make sure you understand, Bernie." Nanan Beha said. "When you get home each day, you are to do your homework, and if you have time, then you may do your chores. But, your homework is what you will do first. Do you understand?" Nanan Beha was waiting for a response.

"Yes, Nanan Beha. I will work hard." I said. Nanan Beha was not upset or angry, and as always, I understood what I had to do. Life was easy when I did what I was told to do. During that extra hour after school, Miss Salas showed me how to work the type of math problem I needed to master. For the rest of the hour I practiced and asked for help if I got stuck. In less than a month I was performing at the top of my class in math. I found out that I loved working with numbers and decided that I wanted to be a bookkeeper when I grew up. When I received a special certificate from Miss Salas for completing the extra math project work, Nanan Beha, Nina Maria, and I celebrated by making homemade ice cream, something we saved for very special occasions.

In the concentration camp I wished that my new life could be as uncomplicated. I tried very hard every day to do what was expected of me. First I learned the soldiers' rules. Early on I noticed a pattern. They woke us at 4:30 in the morning to pray. Then we lined up to ride in the old bus to the rice fields. One soldier rode in the bus while a worker drove the bus. It would have been easy to overtake the soldier, but we knew that our families would be punished for our disobedience. So we just did what we were told.

When Corporal Kikuchi arrived in November 1942, we learned that life could get even more miserable. Corporal Kikuchi was especially vicious. He used a weapon that none of us had seen before: a whip with a wooden handle and thin leather strips with knotted ends.

He frequently snapped his whip to remind us he was in charge—and watching us. Anyone who audibly breathed or whispered would get his attention.

Determined not to be his target, I did not make eye contact with him or anyone else. One afternoon, however, it seemed I was destined for the whip. Corporal Kikuchi sat under the shade of a nearby coconut tree looking bored because no one had been out of line.

Out of the corner of my eye I saw him stand up and leave the only shady retreat the whole field had to offer. I could feel the air crackle as he moved toward us. He yelled in Japanese for us to leave the flooded rice beds. It took a very short time and far too many beatings for us to learn enough Japanese to know when to get up in the morning, when to leave on the tired old bus, and when to begin or end work in the rice fields.

As soon as we heard the solider yell, we all quickly stood up. Several of the older workers could no longer stand erect. They were permanently bent at the waist from working at a 90 degree angle hour after hour, day after excruciating day. Some could no longer squat to do their work because they had spent so much time bending over the river water.

We entered the rice fields by row and also exited by row. Everything was done with precision. On this particular afternoon, the four other workers and I stood up, turned, and started to move toward the bus. One of the older workers, Uncle Reverez, who had worked next to me for nearly two years, suddenly groaned aloud. He had straightened up too fast and his old, weary muscles and bones could not keep up.

Corporal Kikuchi finally had a target. He yelled at the old man. I could see the glee in his face as he licked his lips and squinted his eyes. I immediately looked down. After witnessing many beatings, I knew what was coming next. Not only would Uncle Reverez be beaten, but everyone in the path of the dreaded whip would be hurt as well. The worker on the other side of the soldier's target and I would also feel the whip.

I braced myself for what was coming. Although I had seen several beatings, I had never felt the whip, but I knew that the pain would be intense. I also knew that the only thing that would save me from receiving more of the whip would be to show no emotion. I had watched soldiers thrust the butts of their rifles on the backs of the Guamanian workers and hungrily wait for their victims to scream, a response that prompted the soldiers to injure again.

From where I stood in relation to Uncle Reverez, I was at the end of the whip, so I knew I would not get the slash of the leather straps. Instead, I would receive the unforgiving cuts of the razor-sharp tips. Corporal Kikuchi did not wait until we were out of the rice bed to administer his punishment. He snapped the whip behind him and with the precision of a man who had practiced this movement often, the leather straps sliced the air and hit Uncle Reverez on the middle on his back. I was struck as well as Uncle Sanchez, another older man with a scar on his left arm where he had been shot while working with the Insular Guard. Uncle Sanchez worked on the other side of Uncle Reverez. The knotted tips of the leather whip's blades cut through my shirt and into my back.

Uncle Reverez screamed and dropped into the water. His fall angered

Corporal Kikuchi even more. He motioned for Uncle Sanchez to pull him up, but he let a cry of pain escape. I was determined not to cry out, not to show emotion. I knew what I had to do: continue to look down and grit my teeth to keep the pain to myself. I slowly backed up to merge silently with the row of workers behind me.

I continued to watch Corporal Kikuchi, careful not to meet his gaze. His eyes shone with power and pleasure. As I continued to inch toward the bus with silent determination, I took care to hide my back, now soaked with my own blood. I was glad that my shirt was so dirty.

The trip back to camp was silent—two of the seats newly vacant. I heard whispers that they had been whipped to death and hurriedly buried in shallow graves close to the rice field. Corporal Kikuchi was quick in doing his work for the Japanese Imperial Army.

My fate could have easily been the same. I continued to hide my pain. Somehow once again I had dodged Death's invitation.

ANUFAT, THE TAOTAOMO'NA (ILLUSTRATION BY RAPH UNPINGCO, PRINTED WITH ARTIST'S PERMISSION)

CHAPTER 15

Taotaomo'na

I KNEW WHY THE JAPANESE WOULD NOT TAKE A CHANCE WALKING through the jungle. Uncle Herman told me that they were afraid of the snakes and huge lizards. They also feared that American soldiers might be hiding in the jungle. He smiled.

"Why are you smiling, Uncle Herman?" Seeing his wide, beautiful smile always made me smile too.

"I am smiling because I played a little trick on the soldiers," he said.

"What kind of trick? Was it dangerous? I don't want you doing anything that might make them want to hurt you."

"The soldiers never do anything to hurt me. They all think I am loyal to them—all except Corporal Kikuchi. He is a bad one, that one. I am very careful around him, but the others are gullible and easy to trick.

"Bernie, do you remember how I can make a boonie dog come to me when I call?"

How could I forget the strange whistling noise he made in the back of his throat? Uncle Herman made this noise and almost immediately a boonie dog came out of the jungle. I had never seen anyone call a wild animal before. Uncle Herman could make another sound and the boonie dog would go crazy and start howling and running in circles. The most amazing thing was that you couldn't tell the sounds were coming from Uncle Herman.

"I told several of the soldiers about the Taotaomona and that they do not like people coming uninvited into the jungle. One of the soldiers told me that he did not believe in ghosts and that only fools believed such nonsense." Uncle Herman smiled again. "So I told him I could prove it to him."

"How did you do that, Uncle Herman? How could you prove that the Taotaomona were real?" Anyone who grew up on the island knew that they were nothing to mess with. I was sure that since the Japanese were treating the islanders so badly, the Taotaomona were eagerly waiting for soldiers to enter their territory.

Before Uncle Herman could answer my question, I said, "Did you know that the Taotaomona almost stole me away?" When he shook his head, I continued. "Back in Sumay, I used to help clean the sanctuary. I was so proud that the sisters singled me out and asked me to help every Saturday before the morning Mass. It was my job to sweep the floor. I made sure that every corner and aisle was swept clean and that I did not bump into anything. On this particular Saturday, while I was sweeping the floors, several choir members and one of the sisters entered the sanctuary. I finished sweeping the floor and decided to sit for a while and listen to the choir as they practiced. It was getting late, but I thought if I listened for just a few minutes, I would have plenty of time to get home before dinner. Nanan Beha knew that I was at the sanctuary, cleaning, so she wouldn't be worried.

"I wanted to sing with the choir but was too young. I sat still as Sister Anne, the choir director, gave everyone instructions about the song the choir was going to sing the next day.

"Our Catholic church was one of my favorite places to be. There was little I enjoyed more than the quiet of the sanctuary. Even when I was cleaning the floors, there was a reverence in the room. No one shouted or raised their voices to speak. The only person who spoke above a whisper was the priest when he performed the Mass on Sundays."

"What did you like about the song that the choir sang, Bernie?"

"Uncle Herman, the song I listened to that afternoon was so beautiful and calm; it whispered good feelings to my heart. I watched each member of the choir, and even though some sang high notes and other sang low notes, it was as if they were one voice. I was mesmerized by the music and did not notice how much time had passed. Suddenly the choir stopped singing. I looked through the church windows and saw a gray sky; it was late. I jumped up to leave. Sister Anne, who had not noticed me listening to them, called out, 'Bernie, would you like to sing with us?'

"If I had left at that moment, I probably would have had more than enough time to get home before supper, but I was being asked to sing with the choir and was overcome with joy. I had told the sisters many times that I wanted to sing with them one day and now here was my chance. What an honor!

"I stayed with the choir and sang with them for another hour. Then I knew I had to leave. I said my goodbyes and thanked Sister Anne for allowing me to sing with them and then I started for home. I knew it would take too long to walk home the regular route, but I had a plan. I would just take a shortcut through the tall grass at the edge of the jungle. I knew I was not supposed to go home that way because I could wake up the Taotaomona sleeping in the trees. But at the time, facing the wrath of the unknown felt like a much better choice than facing an angry Nanan Beha." Uncle Herman smiled and sat down. He could tell my story was just beginning.

"I was very quiet. I walked calmly through the tall grass, taking special care not to make much noise. I enjoyed the feeling of the grass against my bare shins. There was a peacefulness as I walked through the grass that I had never felt while walking along the road. I looked up at the branches swaying in the trees. There was a soft rustling as the wind moved the leaves. It was as if each branch was talking. It was like the trees were sharing secrets. The leaves were moving, shaking off the dust of the day and getting ready for the sleep of the night."

Uncle Herman yawned and pretended to be tired and bored.

"I noticed that there were no animals around the trees and in the grass. Usually I would catch a glimpse of a deer, squirrel, or boonie dog running to get home before nightfall. The only sound I heard was the leaves in the trees rustling and the grass gently moving in the wind. I stopped to listen and found myself almost falling asleep. I knew I had to move fast to get home. I fought the strong urge to lie down in the grass and gaze at the stars."

"You felt like lying down in the middle of the jungle at night, Bernie?" Uncle Herman asked, looking incredulous.

"Yes, but I didn't. I arrived at home and stood in the kitchen, smiling from ear to ear because I was on time for dinner. Nanan Beha took one look at me and crossed her arms. Then she asked me a question that surprised me. "'Which way did you come home, Bernie?' Somehow I had a feeling Nanan Beha already knew the answer to her question.

"Uncle Herman, there were times I was convinced that Nanan Beha was a witch. She always seemed to know things. When Nanan Beha asked me the route I had taken home, I knew the best thing to do was to tell the truth. I confessed that I had walked under the trees in the jungle where the Taotaomona sleep. I told her that I was very careful to be quiet and not wake the Taotaomona.

"Then she said, 'Bernie, you were not successful. Look at your bare legs!'

"Uncle Herman, I was so surprised when I looked down at my legs. They were bruised, even though I had not hit them on anything.

Frightened, I screamed, 'What happened to my legs?'

"I didn't have to wait long for Nanan Beha's explanation: 'Bernie, the Taotaomona do not hear with ears like ours. You were lucky that the Taotaomona you awakened were the good spirits and not the bad ones. You were lucky that they wanted only to pinch your legs and not eat them. Tell me everything that happened on your walk home, Bernie. Tell me everything. Do not leave out any details.'

"I told Nanan Beha about how I listened to the quiet and how I felt like lying down on the ground to sleep a while.

"She said, 'Nene, that does not mean that you are not in danger. If they like you, it means that they want you to join them. The only way you can join them is to die. It is good that you did not succumb to their invitation to lie down and sleep with them.'

"Uncle Herman, ever since then, I have truly believed that the Taotaomona exist. But now let's get back to your story. What did you do to prove the Taotaomona are real with the soldiers?"

"I told them that at a certain time in a certain place, the Taotaomona would chase boonie dogs out of the jungle and that the spirits would make the dogs act crazy. Of course, they did not believe me," he chuckled. "So I did my boonie dog call, and as always, one appeared. Then I made the sound that they do not like and it started to howl and to run in circles." Uncle Herman exploded with laughter.

"I told the soldiers that they had better go inside quick because the spirits were very close and they did not like the soldiers. They ran inside so fast that the noise scared the dog away."

Uncle Herman and I laughed so hard that tears streamed down our cheeks. Tired and happy, we walked to our huts to get some sleep.

I lay on my mat, thinking about the joke Uncle Herman had pulled, and smiled again. I knew that the Japanese soldiers were wise to be afraid of the Taotaomona. I had no doubt that any Japanese soldier who was arrogant enough to enter into Taotaomona territory would disappear and never be seen again.

SOLDIERS OF THE IMPERIAL JAPANESE ARMY

CHAPTER 16

———

Fate and Faith

THERE WAS ONE PART OF THE DAY I DREADED MOST—THE BEGIN-
ning. One morning I had a hard time getting up because I had
not slept well. The previous night, I had heard the sound of a whip in
the comfort house. Screaming and crying followed. A couple of hours
passed before I finally fell into a sleep full of dreams about forsaken
girls. I also dreamed about an event from my past—something that
had brought great shame to Nanan Beha but had saved me from suffering the fate of the unfortunate girls in the comfort house. I dreamed
about the day I cut my thick black hair.

Almost every day when I woke, I thanked God for Nanan Beha's punishment. When I heard the girls' screams coming from the comfort house, I knew that I had escaped their fate and wished they had also cut off their hair.

I had also been thinking about a conversation I had with Uncle Herman the evening before. I had asked him to tell me more about the Japanese soldiers.

"Tell me more about the soldiers, Uncle Herman." I enjoyed hearing him talk about the soldiers. After hearing their stories, they seemed more like people than the monsters I saw them as.

"Most of the soldiers are not very interesting. They do their jobs, eat, and sleep. They are easy to understand. The one who is not as easy to understand, though, is the general."

"Why do you say that?"

"General Takahashi is a mystery to me. I have overheard the other soldiers talk about him. He comes from a long line of military men. His grandfather and his father were also in the Imperial Japanese Army, and his brother died with full military honors. But to me he does not seem to have the same feeling toward his life in the military."

"What makes you think that, Uncle Herman?"

"I don't know for sure, but from what I have heard and from the way he treats me, he does not seem to have the heart for the military."

"How does he treat you?"

"General Takahashi told me when I first started working for him that he admired my courage in standing up for our people. At the time,

I thought he might be saying that because he wanted me to trust him so I was suspicious as to his motive. He told me later that he admired people of character. He also told me that before the war started, he was going to tell his father that he was going into the priesthood. Then the war started and he had no choice. He had to join the Army and serve his nation or lose his honor and his family."

"He does not seem to me that he could be a priest, Uncle Herman. How could someone who wanted to be a priest be able to do the terrible things he does?"

"I wonder if he thinks sometimes that he should have also stood up for what he believed was right. He must be fighting in his heart all the time," Uncle Herman said.

Uncle Herman had to go back to his hut then so he could get some rest. I thought more about General Takahashi and how someone who wanted to be a man of God could be in charge of so much killing. Uncle Herman had told me that the Japanese soldiers thought a lot about their honor, but it would be terrible to live a life where every day was a lie. I could not believe it, but I actually felt sorry for the general.

I knew I had to stop thinking about the general and try to get some sleep. The work in the rice fields was difficult for me so I had to get all the sleep I could. It was even harder for Uncle Carlos. His joints and back ached all the time. When the soldier on duty in the rice field was not looking, he tried to stand up straight to relieve his back.

When Uncle Carlos and I first met, we tried not to like each other. We both had lost our families, and neither of us wanted to take a chance on loving and losing again, but it was difficult not to love, especially since we shared our hut together.

Of course, Uncle Carlos knew that I was a girl. His granddaughter, who had been killed in the bombings, had been my age. It was not long before he started telling me stories about the island that he would have told his granddaughter. We both enjoyed these times; they helped us escape—at least in our imaginations. I looked forward to hearing his stories and watched out for him in the rice fields. I felt comfort in knowing that he also watched out for me.

On the morning I dreamed about cutting my hair, the Japanese soldiers were more aggressive than ever. They rattled the gate before they entered the camp and yelled at us to get up. Then they went from hut to hut, shouting commands at those who were moving too slowly.

"立ち上がって, 今動き出せ!" (Get up and get moving now!)

Still drowsy from a short night full of dreaming, I was slower than usual in standing up. Once standing, I started walking toward the center of the camp where we gathered. All I felt was exhaustion from not having slept well the night before.

Usually Uncle Carlos and I left the hut at the same time. As I left this morning, I turned to find him and could see that he was struggling to get up off his thin straw sleeping mat, so I started walking back toward the hut to help him. Before I reached the entrance, Corporal Kikuchi ran over to Uncle Carlos and began screaming at him. Corporal Kikuchi was gesturing wildly and Uncle Carlos was trying to stand and bow, but he was in too much pain to stand erect or to bend his knees and bow. I was about four feet from our hut when I saw Corporal Kikuchi pull his sword from his side. I froze. I saw the fury on his face; his eyes were filled with hate and disgust.

With little hesitation, he raised the sword above Uncle Carlos and dropped his blade, cutting off my dear friend's head and yelling at him all the while. Uncle Carlos' head rolled toward me and his body dropped. When I looked down at my feet, there was his head—his eyes wide open, staring, as if wondering what had happened.

I felt sick. The only reason I did not throw up was that my stomach was empty. I tried to walk, but my legs would not move. Suddenly my head felt very heavy and my legs felt like they were going to give way. Just then, I felt my shoulders lift. Grandmother Lilly came up behind me, put her arm around my waist, and walked me toward the back of the camp. I started to cry. I could not believe what the soldier had done to Uncle Carlos. He had been trying to move, to bow—to do what he was supposed to do. And now he was gone at the hand of a heartless, cold-blooded Japanese soldier who didn't even know this gentle old man's name.

Grandmother Lilly rocked me in her arms, and I cried out, "I hate that soldier. He should die. We should cut off his head too. Uncle Carlos is gone. It took one second and he's gone. I hate that soldier. I hate all of them."

Grandmother Lilly shook her head. With tears streaming down her cheeks, she faced me and placed a hand on each of my shoulders.

"No, Nene. More violence does not help stop violence. You must reach deep inside yourself to your faith and find forgiveness. You must pray that God will help you," she urged.

"I don't feel like praying. I don't want to forgive. How could God let this happen to Uncle Carlos? How could God be a loving God and let all of this happen to Uncle Carlos, to us? Is there even a God? If there is, He has forgotten us."

"I do not know why this is happening, but God has not forgotten us. He will never abandon us. We may not know why this is happening, but it has nothing to do with whether or not God loves us. He always loves us and we must love each other, even the soldiers," Grandmother Lilly continued.

"I cannot love the soldiers. Look what they did to Uncle Carlos and what they do to us every day. How could you love the soldiers? The Japanese killed your family! You should hate them. They are terrible people." I could not believe that Grandmother Lilly was not filled with hate too.

"I do not judge the soldiers, Nene. I miss my family very much, but I have faith that all is happening according to God's plan. I do not know the details of His plan, and I may not understand now—but even so I have faith that it is His plan. You must also have faith, Bernie. Only faith will sustain you, especially now."

I looked at Grandmother Lilly as if for the first time. In the midst of all the killing, starvation, and horror, she always had a peacefulness about her. How could this be?

I hated the soldiers with an overwhelming fury. I was sick with anger and wanted to feel light and whole again. I now saw that Grandmother Lilly could separate herself from the life she was being forced to live and somehow continue to live life on her own terms. I wanted to know how this was possible. If faith was helping Grandmother Lilly understand, then I wanted to understand faith too.

LIEUTENANT GENERAL TAKESHI TAKASHINA,
COMMANDER OF THE 29TH INFANTRY DIVISION, WHO
CAME TO GUAM FROM MANCHURIA IN EARLY 1944

CHAPTER 17

The Enemy

FOR SEVERAL DAYS AFTER UNCLE CARLOS WAS BRUTALLY EXECUTED, I walked around in a daze. Corporal Kikuchi had snuffed out his life as if he had been an annoying insect. I could also not forget how Grandmother Lilly acted after Uncle Carlos was killed. I wanted her to be angry and hate the soldiers as much as I did. I could hardly speak to her without feeling confused and full of rage.

I was angry all the time. I was angry at having to live in a concentration camp, I was angry at having to get up at 4:30 each morning to bow to a god I didn't know and didn't believe in. I was angry that my God had abandoned me. I was angry that there was never enough food. Most of all I was most angry at how calm Grandmother Lilly had remained during and immediately following Uncle Carlos's death.

I just could not understand it. I watched Grandmother Lilly as much as I could throughout the days following Carlos's death. She worked as hard or harder than the other islanders. She had no more food than anyone else. When she was able to get rice, most of the time she gave almost all of it away to others; yet she always seemed at peace. No matter the time of day or the activity, Grandmother Lilly was never out of sorts or upset. I found myself remembering the first days after the bombing. I was completely alone. Nanan Beha and Nina Maria were gone. In my despair God had sent me a guardian angel—Grandmother Lilly. She was my proof that He did exist.

Grandmother Lilly had seen that I had no one and had not left my side since that first day. In the island caves that first night after the bombing, Grandmother Lilly slept nearby. During the days that followed, she gave me enough room to find my way on my own but was always close by and ready with open loving arms. Like me, she had lost everything.

While we lived in the caves, Grandmother Lilly told me of her loss. "After my son, Ian, was born, I lost two children in childbirth. I did not think that God would bless me with another child. Three years later I became pregnant again and was so happy. I felt wonderful and healthy. My pregnancy with my daughter, Atti, went perfectly. Her name means 'one who plays tricks.' True to her name, she was always in some kind of mischief. Her eyes were bright with wonder, and from the time she could walk, I had a terrible time keeping up with her.

"When Ian was three and Atti was just a few months old, my husband, who worked for the hospital, had a terrible accident and was killed. So it was just me and my children. Ian loved his little sister. She could talk him into anything. 'Ian' means 'God is forgiving,' and he was also true to his name. No matter what Atti did, he forgave her."

"You lost your husband too, Grandmother Lilly? You never mentioned that before."

"Yes, Nene. I lost my husband too. He was working the night shift at the hospital. Normally he worked only the day shift, but one night his relief did not come so he had to stay on. During this second shift the hospital lost its electrical power. He had to fix it before he could come home. He was electrocuted when he was trying to fix the problem and died instantly."

"I am so sorry about you losing your husband, Grandmother Lilly. So you had to raise your children by yourself?"

"Nene, I miss my husband, but I have had a lot of help from friends and family. On the day of the first bombing, I was with my two children at the little Catholic church in your village, Bernie. We were visiting my sister who lived in Sumay. Ian, nine at the time, and Atti, six, were playing outside the church while my sister and I helped in the kitchen. Our job was to put food that needed to be kept cool during the Mass in iceboxes.

"Atti was up to her tricks. She kept running away from Ian. Each time she ran away, she got farther away from him. She was having a great time outsmarting him by getting back to the church before he knew where she was.

"The last time Atti ran from him, he came running to me worried because he could not find her. I took his hand and told him to show me where he had last seen her. We were in the tall grass together at the edge of the jungle when the bombs hit the church. I told him to get down on the ground and cover his head and not to come after me as I went in search of his sister. I spotted Atti standing alone by the front door of the church, frozen with fear. I ran towards her—and so did Ian.

He reached her before I did and wrapped his arms around her. As they turned to rejoin me, another bomb hit the ground just in front of the church, killing my little ones and many others who were trying to get away. Their lives were over in seconds.

"I saw nothing left of my Ian and Atti. They were completely gone. Screams from people around me brought me back to my senses, and I started running toward the caves with everyone else."

"That must have been awful for you, Grandmother Lilly. I lost my family too, but I did not see them die. I don't know how I would have been able to live if I had seen them die."

"Nene, it was a terrible day—not just for me but for many of our people. Almost everyone in the village lost a friend or family member. Not a day goes by that I do not think of my sweet, brave Ian and my mischievous Atti."

"Grandmother Lilly, maybe if she had not been so mischievous, she would still be here."

"We are meant to be who we are. I would not have wanted Atti to be anyone else but herself, even if it meant that I would have less time with her."

"But now you do not have her and you have just sadness without her."

"Nene, I do miss my two children, but I do not remember them with sadness. I remember all the joy that they brought into my life. I would do God and myself a disservice if I was not grateful for everything I have. I must live not only for myself but also for others. If the war had not happened, I would not have met you. In the midst of all this sadness, we found each other and already you have given my life such happiness. We need each other to be strong for each other. Life is difficult enough."

Yes, it was. We were all suffering from overwork, lack of sleep, and malnutrition. I was grateful to have Grandmother Lilly in my life, and knew I would not have met her if the bombs had not been dropped.

Certainly she was hungry because she ate less than I did, but I never heard her complain. And of course her back ached from bending over all day and sleeping on the hard ground—but she never spoke of any discomfort. When the other islanders discussed the camp's awful condition and how dreadful their lives had become, Grandmother Lilly did not participate in the conversation.

I had not really paid attention to Grandmother Lilly's demeanor before Uncle Carlos's death. With all that had happened since the bombing, it was hard for me to understand how anyone could be filled with anything but hate. But Grandmother Lilly was filled with love, not hate. I wanted to understand how this was possible. One evening just after everyone had gone to bed, I waited until I heard sounds of sleep coming from inside and outside our hut. I lifted my head and then quietly sat up.

"Grandmother Lilly, are you asleep?" I whispered. Grandmother Lilly's eyes opened slowly. She blinked and lifted her head.

"Not any longer, Bernie. Are you hurt or sick?"

"No, I am not hurt or sick. I don't understand something. That is, I am confused because …" I stumbled over my words, not exactly sure what I wanted to say.

"Take a deep breath, Bernie, and just empty your thoughts."

"On the day Uncle Carlos died, you said you had faith and that I should have faith. It is hard to have faith and believe in anything good anymore. How do you have faith, Grandmother Lilly?"

"I have faith that good is still among us. Although there is so much despair, if you look, you can also choose to see the good," she explained.

"I don't see any good anywhere at all. Where are you looking?" I asked.

"Bernie, like you, I see pain and despair, but there is also good. I look at the magnificence of nature and see the good. I remember I have a choice to see the bad or to see the good. I always have a choice and have faith that all will be well."

I was still confused.

"Look outside the hut, Bernie, and tell me what you see."

I saw the fence topped with the razor-sharp wire and I saw the soldiers' house. I felt the anger welling up in me again. I told Grandmother Lilly what I saw and felt.

"Look again, Bernie. Look beyond what your anger is allowing you to see. Take a deep breath, close your eyes, and when you open them, look again. But this time, look with your heart."

I did as I was told. I closed my eyes and took a long breath. I opened my eyes and looked again. I saw the fence and the razor wire again, but this time I looked through and beyond the fence and I saw the sky. It was the color of blue-black velvet. It was dotted with twinkling stars lighting up the sky. I also saw a bright, full moon. I had not noticed the sky for a long time. I remembered the special times when Nanan Beha and I sat on the porch in silence and looked at the sky. I remembered how good I felt sharing the sky and the silence with Nanan Beha

"What do you see, Bernie?" Grandmother Lilly asked.

"I see the sky."

"What do you see when you look at the sky, Bernie?"

"The sky is so big. It is a pretty color and has stars that look like diamonds. The stars sparkle like Nanan Beha's diamond watch. I like that the sky is so big."

"How do you feel when you look at the sky, Nene? Do you feel angry?"

"No, I don't feel angry. I feel peaceful."

"I also feel peaceful when I look at the sky, Nene. When I see the sky, I feel like I am very small compared to its magnificence. The bad is still here; it does not go away. But wherever I am, I choose to find the good around me instead of the bad. This is the way I nurture hope. My heart cannot feel hope if my mind is closed with anger, hate, and fear."

"I can see good in the sky, but I cannot see any good in the Japanese."

"It is a choice, Nene. Each of us can choose how we look at everything. If we look for despair and misery, we keep the enemy inside of us. There are enemies outside of us, but the enemy we keep inside is far more destructive. It feeds on fear, and anger grows every time we feed it. The enemy inside cannot live in the same body that holds a joyful heart."

I lay back down and thought about what Grandmother Lilly had said. I realized that the enemy was not just the Japanese soldiers but also the hate inside me. I looked at Grandmother Lilly one more time before drifting off to sleep. Instead of thinking about the confining concentration camp, my last waking thought was the brilliance of the twinkling stars in the blue-black sky.

*AT 9:04 A.M. ON SEPT. 2,1945, ABOARD THE BATTLESHIP
USS MISSOURI IN TOKYO BAY, WORLD WAR II ENDED. TWO
CHAMORRO SAILORS WITNESSED THE HISTORIC EVENT.*

CHAPTER 18

Liberation

W E HAD BEEN IN THE CAMP ALMOST THREE YEARS WHEN Uncle Herman noticed that the Japanese soldiers were being more secretive than usual. He sent a message to a cadre of a dozen or so men to meet that evening. Whenever they met, I tried to be close by to grab any bits of news I could.

"You might as well join in, Bernie. Everyone knows you are listening anyway," Uncle Herman said.

"You are taking too much of a risk, Uncle Herman, meeting right here behind Grandmother Lilly's hut," I said one evening when he called an emergency meeting.

"No, Nene. The soldiers are all at a meeting except the one who is standing at the gate," he explained.

"Something is going on, but I cannot tell what. Every day the corporal and sergeants meet with the general in the general's office. They have not done that in the past. The soldiers have suddenly become more guarded and careful about what they say when I am nearby," Uncle Herman said to the others.

"Do you have any idea what this might be?" asked Dale, one of the other translators. Though skinny from three years of malnutrition, somehow Dale was still strong and energetic. One day in the rice fields Uncle Santos passed out and went face down in the river mud. Fortunately, Corporal Kikuchi was not on guard and the soldier who was had wandered off. Even though Dale was not much taller than I was, he quickly carried Uncle Santos and leaned him up against a coconut tree. The old man came to and smiled a silent thank you. Like Uncle Herman, Dale was fearless and kind.

"I heard a portion of one of the messages that came in from another part of the island that said 'no one must survive.' We must warn everyone in the camp to be extra careful not to agitate the soldiers. Whatever is happening or going to happen is upsetting the soldiers," Uncle Herman said. "All other communication from the island has stopped," Uncle Herman continued. He met eyes with all the men and stopped at me. "It is better that we say nothing else about this."

With that, the meeting ended.

Uncle Herman was considered part of the Japanese general's staff. Although he was one of the "savages," the general trusted him. He had to because Uncle Herman was the best translator he had.

"Uncle Herman, I am afraid for you," I said to him after all the other men had left the meeting.

"Don't worry about me, Nene. I am very careful."

"I would feel better if I saw you more."

Uncle Herman went on to tell me how he spent a typical day.

"I cannot risk seeing you too much during the day. Each day I stick to my routine. As soon as I wake, I pull out my rosary that I keep in a hole under my sleeping mat. I know that at 4:30 a.m. I will have to bow to their god with everyone else, but I never fail to say my prayers to my Lord first.

"At 5:00 a.m. I report to the general. I never oversleep and I am never late. During my first week with the general, I learned that he was serious about those under his command following orders. Back in early January 1942, when the soldiers first took over the island and we had settled in Manenggon, my destiny to be a translator was fixed. Early one morning one of the Japanese soldiers was yelling,

'より迅速に移動する!' (Move more quickly!)

"Angry that the old man was not responding, the soldier yelled again and began to shake his fists in the air. Without thinking, I moved between the soldier and the old man and said to the solider, 'He does not understand Japanese.' He was surprised that I could understand

and speak Japanese.

"I told the soldier that I would tell the man to move more quickly—and I did. The old man jumped up and quickly moved. I did not know it at the time, but General Takahashi had watched the entire episode. Within the hour, I was ordered to the general's quarters." Uncle Herman paused.

"Bernie, I am not ashamed to say that I was a little scared. I tried not to show my emotions. The Japanese believe that showing emotion is a sign of weakness. The Japanese general's office was the largest room in the special house. His office and the soldiers' quarters were at the opposite end of the building that also housed the comfort house. The entire structure was quickly constructed from materials brought from the U.S. military bases, where the buildings had been destroyed. The general's office was located at the front of the house. I was brought to the room by a soldier who spit out a command before leaving me in the room alone.

‘あなたが移動するように指示されるまで置かれたまま!’ (Stay put until you are instructed to move.)

"While I waited, I observed the room. It was simply decorated. Green rice wallpaper lined three of the walls. The fourth wall was painted a lighter green. I sat on the floor facing a desk cleared of any papers or objects. Behind the desk was a single chair. Behind the desk was a door. Incense burned in the corner of the room just to the right of the desk. A small statue along with rocks, water in a bowl, and a bamboo plant also sat in the corner along with a stick of burning incense. It looked like an altar of some sort. To the left of the desk was a wooden box. A knife and a machete lay on top. I also noticed that along the wall on my right side was a short table with small rice wine cups and a small plate.

"A few minutes later another young Guamanian boy was brought into the room. He was put on the opposite side of the door to the room on the same wall as me. He was given the same instructions and we were left alone in the room. After a few minutes, he sat on the floor and spoke.

" 'Why do you think we have been brought here?' he asked.

" 'I don't know, but it won't be long before we find out. My name is Herman. What is your name?'

"The frightened young boy replied, 'Joséph.'

"I noticed that he was shaking and kept looking back and forth, first at the door and then at the desk.

"I asked, 'Joséph, how old are you?'

" 'I turned eleven just before the bombings,' he responded.

"Although Joséph was only three years younger than me, I felt as though he was much younger. My mother told me long ago that I had an old soul, but at the time I did not know what that meant. I have always felt different from other boys my age. When I was in school, I met a boy named Jack who had recently emigrated from Japan. I knew that Jack could not be his real name because it didn't sound Japanese at all. His father wanted him to fit in on the island so he gave him an American name." Uncle Herman smiled at the memory and then continued his story.

"Jack's father was a farmer who grew mango, banana, and coconut trees. Jack and I became close friends and enjoyed learning about each other's culture and language. In fact, I spent most of my free time with his family. In the process I learned that there were many Japanese people sprinkled throughout the island. Jack's family included me in their gatherings, and I was comfortable around these quiet, determined, duty-bound people.

"When the island was first bombed in December 1941, my Japanese friends disappeared. I don't know what happened to them, but I believe they are still alive. Perhaps they are hiding in some caves or in the jungle far beyond the reach of the Japanese soldiers. I think about Jack every day; my friendship with him and his family has sustained me during these last three years and helped me not to hate their countrymen. As Joséph and I waited for General Takahashi, I did not feel afraid and tried to help him feel the same.

" 'Joséph, try to relax. It is a distinct disadvantage if you show any emotion. The Japanese consider showing emotion a dishonorable trait.'

" 'I will try, but I am angry and disgusted. I have already witnessed several deaths and none have been for a good reason. Have they brought us here to kill us now?'

" 'If the Japanese wanted to kill us, they would not bring us to the most peaceful, serene place in the camp. They would not contaminate this place with savages they want to do away with.'

"Joséph nodded, relaxed a little, and took a long breath just before General Takahashi stepped into the room. He was not much taller than me. His clothes were clean pressed. I didn't see his shoes, but I bet they were spit-shined. The general pulled the wooden chair out from under the desk, stepped in front of it, and sat down. He did not acknowledge either of us. His short black hair was thinning at the top of his head and his face showed absolutely no emotion. He intertwined his fingers and placed his hands on the top of his desk. Finally he spoke.

" 'My corporal has seen and heard both of you speak Japanese. I will speak to you first in English. Then I will speak to you in Japanese.'

"He looked at me and said,

'あなたは両方を提供できるサービスがあるので，あなたはここで提起されている.'

"Then he asked, 'What did I say just now?'

" 'General Takahashi, you said we have been brought to you because there is a service we can both provide.'

"The general then turned to Joséph and said,

'このリクエストが，順序ではないことを理解していますか?' (Do you understand that this is not a request but an order?)

Joséph nodded but said nothing.

" 'Talk with your mouth, so I can hear you speak,' the general commanded.

" 'Yes, I understand,' Joséph said.

"The general went on to explain that he needed people who could speak Guamanian, Japanese, and English. He also wanted his translators to teach the detainees how to speak Japanese.

"Joséph started to interrupt but stopped when the general held up his hand and said, 'You will not speak to me unless I have asked you to speak.'

"I noticed that Joséph was breathing fast and clenching his fists and that the general had also noticed Joséph's response.

"'As translators you will work for me. You will be on my staff. You will stay in a hut inside the camp, but you will have certain privileges because you work for me. You will follow orders, all orders. If not, you will die. Is this clear?'

"We both said yes. The general yelled a command to the soldier who had been standing just outside the door. The soldier entered and ordered us to exit the room. When we returned to the camp we found that each of us had our own hut, a welcomed luxury. Most of the boys our age had lost their families and had to sleep on the ground without any protection from the elements. Only families were allowed to stay in huts.

"That night, when Joséph and I didn't sleep in our usual places in the open area, people asked us why we were getting special privileges. Joséph ignored their questions. He was just happy to have a separate place where he could be by himself. He immediately retreated to the privacy of his hut.

"I did not sleep in my hut that night. Instead, I walked around the camp, explaining that I had been ordered to be a translator and that I would tell them everything I heard so they would know as much as I did. Only after I had had a chance to explain myself to everyone in the camp did I return to my new hut to sleep. I knew it was important to spend time explaining my new duties to my people."

"You are so smart, Uncle Herman. I don't think I could survive if anything happened to you."

"Bernie, I'm sure that the general does not know who I am in communication with on the island. If he knew, I would have been killed a long time ago. Just this morning I received a message from a Guamanian prisoner in a camp down river that several men escaped from that camp in the middle of the night; they will be relaying messages tonight to all the camps along the river."

"Uncle Herman, how many other camps are there?"

"There are ten that I know of. I will tell you something that I did not tell the others because I did not want them to panic. The Japanese are killing large numbers of our people for no apparent reason."

"Large numbers? What do you mean?"

"Reports from other camps tell me that hundreds are being killed at a time. This past year I have noticed that the soldiers and even the general have been growing tired of the war. But it's not just fatigue I've been noticing the last couple of days. I wonder if there is a connection between the way the soldiers are acting and that so many of our people are being killed en masse. I don't know what is going to happen, but I feel it in my bones that something big is about to happen."

"I think you are right. Lately the soldiers have been disorganized and distracted. The last three days they have let us sleep past sunrise, and I heard that one of the Japanese soldiers ran into the jungle."

"Yes, that was Corporal Hayashi."

"What do you know about him?" I was amazed that Uncle Herman knew so much about the Japanese soldiers.

"It pays to listen, Bernie. Corporal Hayashi is only eighteen years old. He wants to go to school and be a doctor. I overheard another soldier talking about him. He said Corporal Hayashi had not killed anyone yet and did not think he could if he was ordered to."

"It is hard to believe that there are soldiers who have not killed someone. "

"Well, we will never know if he could since he deserted his unit."

"Why do you think he ran into the jungle? Wasn't he afraid of the Taotaomona?"

"I suppose he was more afraid of the evil in front of his eyes than the spirits he might encounter in the jungle."

Uncle Herman told me that the Japanese soldiers were ashamed because Corporal Hayashi deserted them. They would have taken the news better if the corporal had killed himself instead. By running away he brought shame to all. At church I had learned that committing suicide was a sin. In my mind, running away was a much better choice and gave him a chance of getting to heaven.

On July 21, 1944, the soldiers gathered us for a meeting. We tried guessing why. Grandmother Lilly hoped that they were going to give us food that we were told was stored in about three dozen fifty-five-gallon drums that had arrived outside the camp the day before. The young men were ordered to roll five drums to the middle of the open space and to line the rest along the perimeter of the camp inside the fence line. When Herman and his friends finished moving the drums, the soldiers tied the drums together with a small wire.

Even though we all believed these containers held the solution to our hunger, I could not shake the feeling of impending doom. Grandmother Lilly motioned for me to stay close to her as we both walked toward the middle of the camp. The soldiers started yelling and putting the butt of their guns at the backs of the islanders who were moving too slowly. Grandmother Lilly and I were among the last ones to move to the center of camp.

The soldiers started to close the gate. I turned to face the gate and spotted someone moving in the distance. I touched Grandmother Lilly's arm and nodded my head in the direction of the area behind the open gate. I could not believe what I saw: three American soldiers hiding in the bushes. One of the American soldiers was gesturing for those of us who had noticed them to keep quiet and not let the Japanese soldiers know that they were there, but it was too late. Another Guamanian spotted the Americans and started jumping up and down, yelling, "We are saved!"

The Japanese soldiers turned and started shooting at the American soldiers. As they returned fire, the Americans shouted for us to get down. Many Guamanians dropped to the ground, but countless others turned to the Japanese and attacked them with their bare hands. Several Guamanian were killed in the crossfire.

I dropped to the ground and covered my head with my arms. I lay next to Grandmother Lilly, praying for the shooting to stop. After thirty minutes it finally did. I raised my head. All the Japanese soldiers lay dead on the ground. Many of our people were also dead. The remaining islanders ran to the Americans, hugging them as if they were old friends, thanking them and praising God.

Our rescuers told us that by the next day the Americans were going to bomb the island to kill the Japanese and that we needed to leave and to go to hide in a safe place. Some Guamanians ran toward the jungle. Most of us chose to return to the caves, a longer trip than the jungle but safer by far. I found Grandmother Lilly and together we ran toward our refuge. In the distance we could hear one of the American soldiers shouting, "More Americans will be arriving soon, but be careful. The shooting is not over. This time it will be coming from the sky." Uncle Herman also escaped but only stayed long enough to tell me and Grandmother Lilly that he would join us in the caves later.

Just as the soldier had warned, the fighting was not over. We hid in the cave for two weeks, listening to bombs drop and small groups of American and Japanese soldiers shoot each other. On the fourteenth day Uncle Herman came to us to tell us that the war was finally over. He said that thousands of American and Japanese soldiers were dead, but finally the Japanese no longer controlled the island. One month away from my eleventh birthday, I dropped to my knees, clasped my hands, and looked to the heavens. The war was over, and I had survived.

CHAMORRO CHILDREN CROWD THE STREET OF THIS
CAMP IN AGANA. THE SHELTERS WERE MADE FROM
SHEETS OF CORRUGATED TIN ROOFING.

CHAPTER 19

Reunion

EVEN AFTER THE BOMBING STOPPED, WE STAYED IN THE CAVES. Was it really safe to leave? Did we dare believe we were really free? Though we were uncertain who we would find and how we would begin our lives again, our eagerness to start searching for loved ones who had been taken to different camps finally pushed us out of the cave. When I had first arrived at the concentration camp in Manenggon three years earlier, I was one of three thousand detainees. When Uncle Herman came to the cave to let me and Grandmother Lilly know it was time to leave, he told us that that no one yet knew how many of those had died from disease or starvation and how many had been killed by the soldiers. All we knew was that we were free and safe at last.

"When you and I were talking about the mood being different at the camp, the soldiers had received orders to kill all of us. When the soldiers ordered us to move the drums, they were luring us to our deaths with promises of food. The drums were actually filled with dynamite. Their plan was to detonate the explosives once they were all out of the camp. If the Americans had not arrived when they did, we would all be dead. We have a long way to go to rebuild a new life and we must get to it."

And we did. Many of us returned to our former homes to start the rebuilding process. Since she had lost her family, Grandmother Lilly returned to Sumay to live with me. The only thing still standing was the five-foot cross outside the Catholic church, a sign that our faith had gotten us through this terrible time.

For the next three years we took slow steps to start over. With help from the Americans, we built homes, a school, a church, and a small store. Following our liberation, we did not hold our customary cele-brations. We needed time to grieve all that we had lost.

As we rebuilt our lives, Uncle Herman did not live with me and Grandmother Lilly but did visit at least once a month. He did not give us any details about his activities except that he was traveling across the island and working with the Americans to help Guam regain its strength. Like everyone else, I was trying to start a new life, but memories of the war remained in the back of my mind. Even so, some things changed. For one, I was grateful for every single day of freedom. I thanked God for my life, my village, my food, and most of all for Grandmother Lilly and Uncle Herman. I took nothing for granted.

Grandmother Lilly and I worked hard together to help rebuild our village. She supervised the building of our coconut leaf house. Many of the islanders had lived in such houses before the war, so it was not unusual to do so after our return. Of course, our new homes would be very different from our small, miserable huts; our new homes would have four sides, a roof, and a door. After living through the challenging times during the war, everything now felt like a luxury. We could come and go as we pleased.

In time the coconut, banana, and mango trees bore fruit. And finally we could enjoy the bounties of the ocean—fish, crab, and shrimp. The Americans also shared their canned rations. Spam, a processed ham, was my favorite.

Grandmother Lilly encouraged me to talk often about the past or whatever was bothering me. She told me it was better to discuss the pain rather than let it fester and become an angry force inside. One night after our evening meal, I asked Grandmother Lilly how old her children would be and what memories she had of them.

"Atti would now be nine. She had the most beautiful face, an angel's face. And Ian, my little man, would be twelve. He was always thinking things through." Grandmother Lilly's face looked happy.

"Why are you not sad when you talk about them? I still don't understand."

"Memories of my children do not make me sad, Bernie. I was blessed to have Atti and Ian in my life. If I only cried and was sad when I remembered them, I would make my memories of them sad too. My little ones were never sad. Besides, I know I will see them again in heaven. When I do, we will be so, so happy to see each other."

"Grandmother Lilly, how do you know there is really a heaven? Joshua at the village store says there is nothing after we die and that all we do is rot in the ground. He said there is no proof that there is a heaven."

"Heaven is not in the mind, Bernie. Those who search for heaven in the pages of a book will never find it. Heaven, like faith and hope, comes from the heart. Not the part of the heart that pumps our blood in our bodies but from a different place in the heart."

"I don't know, Grandmother Lilly. Joshua makes a lot of sense because it is difficult to believe what we can't see."

"The best part of life is not what we see; it's what we feel. Let me help you understand, Bernie. Think about a butterfly. The butterfly is not born as a butterfly. It starts out as a caterpillar crawling on its belly to find food. Then it wraps itself into a cocoon, a safe house. After a couple of weeks, it emerges as a very different creature—a beautiful, fragile, and colorful butterfly. The kind of miracle that allows this to happen is only a small sample of the power of God and His universe. I don't think a God who makes this kind of beauty would create life that ends at death. I believe that He created life to continue for all time."

Grandmother Lilly had a wonderful way of helping me to understand. Although she wasn't really my grandmother, I felt at home calling her that.

I was fourteen years old when Grandmother Lilly and I attended our first post-war salt-making party. To make the salt we started three large fires on the shore early in the morning. We placed a metal tripod on each fire and atop those put cast iron pots. Children were responsible for carrying buckets of salt water from the ocean. Adults poured them into the pots on the open fires. As the water boiled, we took turns stirring it, fetching more water, playing music, eating, and sleeping on the sand all through the night and into the morning. The old ladies sang and danced, and the men drank fermented coconut milk and played songs on their guitars, ukuleles, and harmonicas. The meat of the coconut left over from the fermentation process was dried and used to make my favorite sweet treat, ahu. By early morning each of the pots had several cups of clean, pure salt.

For breakfast we set up tables halfway between the ocean and our homes. We had to walk only about twenty-five feet from our house to the tables on the beach. I was helping put plates of food on the table when Grandmother Lilly came over to me. She had a very serious expression on her face.

"Is something wrong, Grandmother Lilly?"

"Nene, come with me. I need to talk with you in private." She led me around to the back of our house. Although I was a teenager, I still enjoyed when she called me Nene. I followed her outside. She sat on a stump outside the house and motioned for me to sit next to her.

"Have you thought of your family since we returned to Santa Rita?"

It was still strange for me to think of my village as Santa Rita, but since Sumay had been destroyed, the island leaders thought it best to give our new village a new name.

"No, Grandmother Lilly, I have not thought much about my family." To manage my sadness during the war, I often daydreamed about my life before the war. Now I tried not to think about everything and everyone I had lost. Instead I focused on the living and the good—just as Grandmother Lilly had taught me.

"We have news for you, Bernie. It's about Nina Maria and Nanan Beha," Grandmother Lilly continued. "Someone is here to see you."

At that moment, Uncle Herman walked up, and I ran to greet him. Even though I had seen him each month since the Americans had liberated Guam, it was not nearly often enough. I knew he was very busy doing his part to restore order to our island. Because of all we had endured during the war, I felt a strong attachment to him. At the same time, I was curious about the urgency of Grandmother Lilly's manner.

"You look well, Bernie. You no longer look like a boy. I see you decided to let your hair grow," Uncle Herman said.

"Yes, Uncle Herman, I have. My short hair served a useful purpose during the war, but now I want a new life and a new look."

I no longer found it a bother to brush and braid my hair every day, and now that we always had access to fresh water, I enjoyed washing it. Time and circumstances had changed my outlook on so many things.

The conversation did not seem to match the concerned feelings Grand-mother Lilly was showing. Finally I asked him whether he was all right.

Herman nodded his head. "Yes, Bernie, I am fine. I have been very busy working with the Americans to locate missing relatives and friends of the Guamanian survivors. I enjoy my work reuniting families and friends. You didn't know, but my top priority has been to locate your family."

"You have been trying to locate my family?" I asked. "But, all my family died on the first day of the bombing."

Herman looked at Grandmother Lilly first and then at me. "No, Bernie. Not all your family died.

"On the day of the bombing, Nanan Beha and Nina Maria were not in the church, as we originally thought. For some reason, just before Sumay was bombed, they left the church and were walking toward Agana. We don't know why, but it does not matter. What does matter is that they survived, Bernie. Both survived!"

I could not believe it. I was fourteen and had last seen them just after my eighth birthday. During all that time I thought I had lost them.

"Bernie, I must tell you that Nanan Beha suffered much pain during the war. Several times she refused to bow and pray to their god. The beatings she suffered have left her weak and unable to speak or walk very well. Nina Maria posed with a man as her husband to save her from the comfort house. She, like many Guamanians, was malnourished during the war, but she is in better health now."

"I can't believe it, Uncle Herman. I just can't believe it. All this time I had hoped they were alive. And now I'm finding out that they are."

"They are arriving here tomorrow. We will build another house so that you, Nanan Beha, and Nina Maria can live together once more.

You will still be close to Grandmother Lilly."

The following morning at eight, Uncle Herman fulfilled his promise. He brought Nanan Beha and Nina Maria to Santa Rita. I was sitting in front of the house I shared with Grandmother Lilly. Eager to see Nanan Beha and Nina Maria again and worried about leaving Grandmother Lilly all alone, I had not slept much.

As I sat waiting that morning, Grandmother Lilly read my mind. "Bernie, I want you to know that you will always have a home here with me. You must not feel bad about leaving me here, and you don't have to stay with me just because you don't want me to be alone. I am never alone."

"But, Grandmother Lilly, you have no one left." I could not bear it if she was ever lonely or felt sad.

"Oh, Bernie," she said with a smile and a twinkle in her eyes. "I am so blessed. Just because you or my children are not with me does not mean that I'm alone. Every time I see the beauty in a plant or animal, I see the beauty and wonder that was also in my children and that is in you. We are all connected, and when they left this earth, they did not take their love with them. It is forever in my heart. When there is love, there cannot be loneliness. Your Nanan Beha needs you to show her the love that you have shown me." As always, Grandmother Lilly helped me feel better.

In the distance, I saw three people walking towards our house. Nina Maria spotted me first and started running toward me. I ran toward her too. We met halfway, laughing and crying. She held my face in her hands, repeating prayers of thanks.

"I cannot believe it is you. It is really you, Bernie? We thought you had died. I still cannot believe we did not lose you."

I turned to see Nanan Beha walking slowly toward me. I was glad that Uncle Herman had prepared me for how different Nanan Beha would look. She was slumped over and had to strain to look up at me. I had seen Nanan Beha sick only once. Before the war, we were preparing a bat for one of the Americans, and the chemicals she was using made her feel nauseated.

"Do you need to see a doctor, Nanan Beha?" I asked her.

"No Bernie, I am fine. I'll just rest a minute in the fresh air. It's not good to pamper a sickness."

"What do you mean, Nanan Beha?"

"I mean, there are people who allow their pain or sickness to become who they are. They lose track of their true self and become the disease. No good comes from dwelling on pain or sorrow."

As I reached to hug Nanan Beha, I saw that her dear face was filled with pain. Sorrow had made Nanan Beha a different person, but that did not matter. We were together again. I was thrilled to have her back under any condition.

Neighboring Guamanians and some American soldiers helped us build our new house, which was only a little ways from Grandmother Lilly's house. I had big responsibilities in my new home, but I stopped by Grandmother Lilly's house at least once a day to help her out and enjoy her company.

My life was complete. I was reunited with the only family I knew. After everything I had lived through, life would be easy now, wouldn't it? Although the war with the Japanese was over, my internal war, filled with memories of the past, continued to haunt me for many years.

*A GROUP OF GUAMANIAN MEN SHOW THEIR JOY
AT HEARING THE NEWS OF JAPAN'S SURRENDER.*

CHAPTER 20

Decisions

WE WERE TOGETHER AGAIN—ME, NANAN BEHA, AND NINA Maria. Nanan Beha had changed a lot. She remembered me, but her spirit was severely damaged. She was afraid of everyone and everything and would not leave our house except to attend Mass. When we were first reunited, she could barely speak. As we spent more time together, she became more verbal. Nina Maria was now our main breadwinner. She worked at the village grocery store and continued selling her baked goods and sewing. She was so busy that Nanan Beha and I rarely saw her.

I wanted to get a job and help make money too, but Nina Maria said I needed to stay with Nanan Beha because it was not safe to leave her alone. Before the war, Nanan Beha had been a strong, independent woman. Living in the camp had transformed her; she was suspicious and hateful and depended on me and Nina Maria for everything. If I was a few minutes late from school or church, I got a lecture. She did not like our neighbor who stayed with her while I was away. Nanan Beha had lost her spirit, her faith, herself; she was like a stranger to me.

One day I went to the store to get some island sweet bread, a treat that Nanan Beha liked. She gave me strict instructions to go to the store, purchase the bread, and then return home. When I arrived at the store and stood in line to pay, a woman standing behind me tapped me on the shoulder and asked me how my new niece was doing.

I was surprised at the question. "I beg your pardon, Ma'am."

"Your new niece. I just heard your sister had a baby girl. How is she doing?"

"I'm sorry. You must have mistaken me for someone else. I don't have a sister," I said with a sick feeling in my stomach.

"Are you Bernidita, who lives with Maria? She is your godmother, right?"

"Yes, I'm Bernidita, and Nina Maria is my godmother, but I don't have a sister or a niece." I didn't recognize the woman. And I was relieved when she stopped talking to me. After I paid for the bread I ran home. Nanan Beha was sleeping when I got home. I did not want to wake her. I had to sit with my confusion until Nina Maria came home at suppertime. While I waited, I cooked supper in case Nanan Beha woke up and was hungry.

As soon as Nina Maria walked in the door, I told her what had happened at the store.

"I was standing in line at the store today. Nanan Beha sent me there to get the bread that she likes so much. You should learn how to bake that bread, Nina. I am sure it would be better than what we buy and it would cost less too."

"I think it is better that we buy the bread, Bernie. Mama is very particular about her bread. I would not like to be responsible for not baking it the way she likes it."

"Well, anyway, I was standing in line and a woman behind me tapped me on the shoulder."

"A woman? Did you recognize her, Bernie? What did she look like, Bernie?"

"She was about your height and weight, about thirty-five or forty years old. I don't remember much about her because I tried to ignore her and not listen to her."

"Why? You were not disrespectful, were you Bernie?"

"No, I was not disrespectful, but I felt uncomfortable about what she said to me."

"What in the world did she say that made you feel uncomfortable?"

"She asked me how my sister was doing. She said my sister had just had a baby and that now I was an auntie."

Nina Maria had been drinking from a cup. She coughed and choked and sprayed the liquid from her lips and spilled it all over the front of her blouse. She stood up suddenly.

"Are you okay, Nina?"

"Yes, I am fine. She said you have a sister?"

"Yes, she said I have a sister who just had a baby. I kept telling her she was mistaken, but she would not stop saying it. Is something wrong?"

Nina Maria looked very nervous and coughed a little to clear her throat. "No, umm, nothing is wrong." She sat down and then said, "Do you remember much about your life before you came to live with us, Bernie?"

"No. During the war I thought a lot about Nanan Beha and you, but I don't remember much before my life in Sumay. I remember feelings I had when my mama held me, but that's pretty much it."

I stood up to leave the room and did not notice that Maria was watching me.

Later in the week I noticed that a girl about my age was following me home from school. I had not seen the girl before in Santa Rita. Each day, whether I took a short cut or a longer way home, she stayed with me. Finally I stopped, turned around, and confronted her.

"Who are you and why are you following me?"

At first the girl did not say anything. She just stared at me. "My name is Connie. I live north of here in Agana."

"Why are you following me? Am I supposed to know you?" I asked.

"I don't think you know me, but I know you."

"Why do you know me?"

"I know you because you are my sister. I am following you because someone should tell you that you have sisters and a brother," the girl blurted out.

"You are lying. I don't have any sisters or brothers." I had that sick feeling in my stomach again. "I live with my Nanan Beha and Nina Maria, and we don't have any other family."

"Bernie, I am your sister. I am two years older than you. You also have two more sisters older than you and an older brother. You are my baby sister. I am telling you the truth."

"Leave me alone and stop following me!" I ran home crying. When I arrived home, I ran into the kitchen. Uncle Herman was sitting at the kitchen table talking with Nanan Beha when I burst through the kitchen door.

Nanan Beha said, "Bernie, watch your manners. You don't come running through the house like a wild animal. Why are you crying? Sit down, calm yourself, and then tell me what is wrong." Sometimes I was not sure it was a blessing that Nanan Beha had gotten her voice back.

I told her and Uncle Herman about the woman in the grocery store and the girl who followed me and how they both insisted I had a family.

"The girl's name is Connie. She said that I have two other sisters and an older brother. Why is she telling me this?"

Nanan Beha took a long breath. Uncle Herman started to speak, and then Nanan Beha held up her hand, gesturing for him not to say anything. "No, Herman, I should tell her."

"They are telling you the truth. You do have a family other than me and Nina Maria. When your mother died giving birth to Manny, your brother who also died, your grandparents could not care for you. Maria, my daughter and your godmother, raised you. You know this is our way on the island."

I was shocked. I waited a few minutes and then said, "But why didn't you tell me? Why didn't you tell me that I have three sisters and a brother? Why did I have to find out this way?" I was hurt and confused.

Nanan Beha was quiet. She did not say anything. Herman then spoke. "Nanan Beha, I must tell Bernie everything now." I looked at him and thought that there could not possibly be any more secrets.

He faced me and said, "Bernie, I am not just your friend. I am ... " He took another long breath. "I am your brother. When our grandparents gave you to Nanan Beha and Maria, I left our family and moved to Sumay to make sure I could keep an eye on you. We had cousins there, so it was easy for me to move in with them to watch out for you. When the war began, I made sure I was nearby, so that I could stay in the same concentration camp."

"But why didn't you tell me about all this, Uncle Herman?" I asked. I began to think back through the days before, during, and after the war. I remembered whenever I needed anything he was always in the right place at the right time. "Why didn't you tell me?" I asked again.

"Before the war, I was told not to say anything to you. Nanan Beha said she would pick the right time. I respected her wishes. During the war, it was too dangerous for anyone to know that you were my sister. The Japanese would have used you to blackmail me. Both your life and my life would have been in danger. There was no good time during the war to tell you the truth about your family. I came here today to appeal to Nanan Beha that you must know the truth. And you know you don't need to call me 'Uncle' anymore."

I was speechless. I had always wanted a large family, but I had let go of that dream long ago. And now my dream had come true.

I turned to my brother and asked, "Will you tell me about my sisters?"

"You have three sisters: Betty is twenty-three, Mary is twenty-one, and Connie is sixteen. Ever since Mama died, Betty has been in charge. At first Betty and Mary lived with Nanan Juna, our father's mother. When she died only a few years later, our three sisters went to live with Nanan Colsa, Mama's mother."

"Nina Maria told me that Nanan Colsa may not like that I am returning to Agana."

"Yes, Bernie. I talked with Maria also. Nanan Colsa is still a bitter person but she is harmless. You will be busy getting to know your sisters, so she won't have time to bother you."

"I hope not. Nina Maria told me that Nanan Colsa was always after someone with her cane in the past, so to watch out for that."

"That's still good advice but I think she does that to keep people away from her more than to hurt people. She keeps to herself most of the time. Our sisters Betty and Mary run the house. Betty did a good job raising us. She started working very young so she could help support our family. She got married about two years ago, but she and her husband chose not to move out and live in their own home. They still live at Nanan Colsa's house. She could not leave our other sisters. Betty has recently had a baby, a girl named Lillian." This meant that I was really an auntie, just like the woman in the store had said.

Herman continued, "Your next oldest sister, Mary, thinks she is a princess. She does not like to work and is waiting for a man to provide a life of luxury for her. She is a dreamer. I am next and then there is Connie. You have already met Connie.

"Connie is used to getting her own way. Once she makes her mind up to do something, there is no stopping her. Mary and Connie still live in our home in Agana." Herman went on to explain that my sisters wanted me to live with them. "They want to make up for lost time and get to know their little sister. Connie is especially excited about the possibility of your moving to Agana."

I wanted to visit them but was not sure how Nanan Beha was going to like the idea of my leaving. As if reading my thoughts, Herman told me that he had already talked with Nanan Beha and that he had arranged a time for me to visit my siblings. After that I could decide where I wanted to live. As we talked more, I realized that it would be strange but I didn't need to call him "Uncle" anymore. So much had changed in such a short time. It was past dinnertime when he left.

I sat alone, my mind swirling with all the news. Move to Agana? How could I leave Grandmother Lilly, Nanan Beha, and Nina Maria? But, oh, how I wanted to meet and spend time with my sisters.

I went in search of Nanan Beha and found her sitting outside on the bench in our front yard. I did not say anything. We both sat in the dark until finally Nanan Beha said, "You must not leave me, Bernie. I know you want to get to know your family, but you must stay with me. You cannot leave. I forbid it!"

I was surprised by her attitude but did not say anything. I wanted to talk with Nina Maria about this news, so I waited until she came home from work. When she arrived, I talked very fast and told her all about Herman's visit. She did not look surprised.

"I know about your family, Bernie."

"You knew too? How could everyone I know keep this kind of information from me?"

"Nanan Beha wanted to protect you. Your Nanan Colsa was very powerful in Agana. Mama did not want to take a chance that she would lose custody of you. The living conditions were not good when you stayed with your Nanan Colsa. Nanan Beha gave us strict orders not to say anything to you. She wanted you to grow up in a clean, loving, orderly home where you could be cared for properly. She was doing what she thought was best for you."

"She has forbidden me to leave, Nina." I am so confused.

"You must do what is best for you, Bernie. I wish I could make this easier, but you will have to decide."

The next day I stopped by Grandmother Lilly's home to talk with her. I told her all about what I had learned about my sisters and that Herman was my brother.

"I knew there was something special about Uncle Herman ... I mean Herman. He was always there for me. We had a special bond from the beginning. Did you know he was my brother, Grandmother Lilly, and that I had sisters?"

"Not then, Bernie. I didn't know until yesterday. Herman came by to see me after he had told you. It was wise of him not to tell anyone during the war. It would have been dangerous had the soldiers found out that you were brother and sister."

I also told her what Nanan Beha had said about me moving to Agana.

"What do you want to do, Bernie?"

"I have always wanted to have a big family, Grandmother Lilly. Now I feel like God has given me a chance to have what I have wished for, but I can't leave Nanan Beha with her feeling like this. I love her and she has done so much for me. She would be very unhappy."

"How would you feel if you did not go, Bernie?"

"I would be sad and wonder about my sisters and what I lost in not getting to know them."

"You must do what you feel in your heart is the best for you, Bernie. Nanan Beha is speaking from fear now, but in her heart she knows you must go. If you make the decision to stay, you will grow to resent her, and deep down she knows that too."

"But I owe so much to Nanan Beha, Grandmother Lilly."

"Your life is your own, Bernie. Your choice on whether to stay or go should not be based on guilt."

I decided not to spend time now worrying about the decision. First I wanted to meet my sisters. Herman was going to come by in the morning and take me to Agana.

Before I closed my eyes to go to sleep that night, I thought about the next day. I was looking forward to meeting Betty, Mary, and Connie, and my baby niece, Lillian. The next morning I went to Nanan Beha to tell her what I had decided.

"Nanan Beha, I am leaving today to spend the weekend with my sisters and my niece. I love you very much and I am grateful for all that you have taught me. I am going to visit my sisters only to meet them. I will return on Monday. I want to meet them before I make a decision whether or not I want to stay and live with them. "

"Bernie, I do not want you to go. I thought I had lost you during the war. I don't want to lose you again."

"Nanan Beha, you are not losing me. You will never lose me. I will always love you, and I will always consider you and Nina Maria as my family. But this is something I must do."

"I understand. I don't like it, but I understand. You have my blessing to visit your sisters, Bernie." Nanan Beha looked so sad.

"I'll be back on Monday, Nanan Beha. Nina Maria told me that you have decided to open our home for a girl who needs a family. I will meet her next week when I return home."

I was hoping that the invitation to invite an orphan into our home would help Nanan Beha back on the road to her old self. Nina Maria told me that Nellie, age fourteen, had spent three years in one of the comfort houses. Nina Maria told me that Nellie and Nanan Beha needed each other and that I needed to meet the family I did not know I had.

WORLD WAR II MEMORIAL TO THE PEOPLE OF GUAM

CHAPTER 21

———

Choices

AFTER STAYING WITH MY SISTERS FOR ONE WEEKEND, I DECIDED to follow my heart and live with them. I thought it was going to be difficult saying goodbye to Nanan Beha, but she had already started trying to make a life for Nellie. So on the day I left to live in Agana, Nanan Beha was in much better spirits that I thought she would be. I hugged her and Nina Maria, kissed them both, and then climbed into the oxen cart. Uncle Herman and I were making the short trip together to Agana.

My sisters and I all lived together in Agana with Nanan Colsa. There were times when I questioned my decision to leave Nanan Beha, but building my relationship with my brother and three sisters turned out to be the right decision. Once a month I returned for a weekend to visit Nanan Beha and Nina Maria in Santa Rita. Of course I also visited Grandmother Lilly.

Nanan Colsa was very different from Nanan Beha and Grandmother Lilly. It was probably a good thing that I did not remember anything from the time I lived with her, before I moved to Sumay. She never had a kind word for me and was always trying to hit me with her cane. Thankfully, most of the time she hardly acknowledged my presence. However, I always had a kind smile for her and tried to make her laugh. I enjoyed the challenge because smiling was not one of the things that Nanan Colsa did often. During one of my visits back in Santa Rita, after I had poured my heart to her, Grandmother Lilly helped me understand my grandmother.

"Sometimes I question why I chose to live at Nanan Colsa's house. At first she barely paid any attention to me at all. Now, she goes out of her way to make me feel unwelcome. She is so mean. I have to watch out for her all the time with that cane of hers. Why are some people born so mean anyway?"

"Bernie, I don't think anyone is born mean. Have you noticed that your Nanan Colsa limps?"

"Yes, Grandmother Lilly, I noticed. I think she limps because she was beaten during the war."

"Yes, she was beaten during the war, but she was crippled long before the war began. As a small child, her grandmother beat her often, so often that her legs were permanently damaged. Your Nanan Colsa must have been very strong not to appear weak during the war because as you know, the soldiers removed old, crippled people because they hated weakness."

"I didn't know that about Nanan Colsa. Why do people do such things to children?"

"I don't know all the reasons, Bernie, but I do know that we do things for a reason. We may not understand why at the time, but there's always a reason. If you take the time to understand this, it's easier to get along with those around you. Do not judge, Bernie. Instead, strive to understand and accept people for who they are."

I tried to remember my conversation with Grandmother Lilly when I was with Nanan Colsa. The more I tried to understand her, the easier it was to be around her. I started to understand that she was more sad than angry and what she yearned for most was solitude, so I tried to stay out of her way. Most of the time that worked. It was hard trying to figure out what she wanted, but I didn't care how difficult it was to live with Nanan Colsa as long as I could be with my sisters.

Betty was a self-taught photographer who took photos for the local newspaper. When she first started working at the paper, she caught the eye of the editor of the newspaper. It wasn't long before their relationship blossomed. Shortly after they met, they got married and started having children. She didn't stop until she had a dozen. I was her favorite babysitter. I adored my nieces and nephews and never said no when asked to take care of her children. I wanted very much to have a large family of my own one day.

Mary, my prettiest sister, was a wonderful organizer, and in our home this skill was definitely needed. Our home was crowded since Nanan Colsa, Betty, her husband Jerry and their children, Mary, Connie, and I all lived there. Mary didn't do any of the work around the house, but because of her supervision, all meals were cooked on time, the house was clean and we always stayed within our budget.

As a young teenager, Mary started fantasizing about finding a prince. At age twenty-two , soon after I moved in, she found her prince, a local politician, and got married. She gave Nanan Colsa two grandchildren, a girl and a boy. When Nanan Colsa asked Mary if she was going to have more children, Mary said with a laugh, "No, I have given you a boy and a girl—that's all they come in!" Mary was finished having children.

Connie was closest in age to me, and we were inseparable. I didn't think I could ever be so close to another human being. She told me that she remembered me before I moved to Sumay and was very sad when I left Agana.

"It was a terrible day. I was seven years old and you were five. I dropped by Nanan Colsa's to visit you. Betty, Mary, and I did not live with you. After you were born prematurely, both you and Mama were very weak. The two of you lived with Nanan Colsa to give you a chance to get stronger. Betty, Mary, Herman, and I lived with Mama's cousins. When Mama got pregnant again, she became very ill and died right after giving to birth to Manny, who died soon after she did. In another month, Daddy died too. You stayed with Nanan Colsa, and the rest of us went to live with Nanan Juna, Daddy's mother. She was so kind to us, but Nanan Juna was too old to take care of all of us, so you had to stay with Nanan Colsa, Mama's mother. It was a hard time after Mama died. We all missed her so much. It is still hard to talk about it, even after all this time," Connie said. She stopped and blew her nose and wiped the tears from her eyes.

Then she continued, "I always looked forward to visiting you at Nanan Colsa's house. Even though I was only seven and you were five, I felt like I needed to take care of you. I held your hand whenever we walked together. I combed and brushed your hair and helped you get ready for bed. We said our prayers together. My other sisters were older than me and I felt so much closer to you. Then the day you moved to Sumay, Nanan Colsa told me you had gone to live with Nina Maria. Herman moved to Sumay to stay with cousins so he could keep an eye on you. I refused to eat for a week. I was heartbroken. Nanan Colsa and Nanan Juna were so worried about me. I thought about you all the time. Shortly after you left, Nanan Juna died and we moved in with Nanan Colsa. Then the war broke. During the war, I received word from Herman that you had survived. We lost touch with Herman after that, but knowing that you were alive kept me alive."

Connie and I made up for lost time. We weren't just sisters. We were best friends. We went to dances together at the church. We shared a room and sometimes talked through the night. I think we were trying to have all the conversations we would have had had if we had grown up together. We shared clothes, shoes, books—everything. She taught me how to put on make-up. She had learned some tips on being a photographer and had often helped Betty with taking photographs. Connie was always taking my picture. She and I looked like we could have been twins. The only big difference between the two of us was Nanan Colsa's attitude toward us. Nanan Colsa adored Connie. She didn't feel the same about any of my other sisters, Herman or me. Because Connie and I were so close, Nanan Colsa left me alone. We remained close even when she married a military man who was stationed in the United States.

Living in Agana gave me a chance to know Herman even better. He felt responsible for me and I for him. When he left the island at twenty-one, he joined the U.S. Navy and never failed to send money and cards to me from his many duty stations.

I visited Santa Rita every month. Nina Maria married a retired military man and together they had two girls. Having grandchildren of her own transformed Nanan Beha to the woman she had been before the war. She was no longer a sad, fearful woman. Her grandchildren were the light of her life. Helping Nellie also softened her heart. I knew she was going to be just fine.

My life was normal for a seventeen year old on the island. I graduated from high school and was active at church. I worked at the church as a housekeeper. My life was simple and predictable and I loved it. Everything completely changed, however, when I met Joe

Santini, an airman in the U.S. Air Force, at church one Sunday. We were immediately attracted to each other. Shortly after we met, Joe asked for permission to court me. Even though I was almost eighteen, we adhered to the island's courting customs. Nanan Colsa accompanied us everywhere we went. We were never allowed any time alone. I knew Joe cared for me because he somehow tolerated Nanan Colsa's sarcastic, hateful attitude toward him.

Joe loaded aircraft at the military base. He had been in the Air Force for only two years when we met and fell in love. He called me his "island flower." Every day for months, chaperoned by Nanan Colsa, we took long walks, sat and talked, or sometimes just sat. Joe was an outsider, and my family was reluctant to allow the courting. However, Joe's natural charm won me over, and I was determined to be with him.

Joe's easy humor and childlike playfulness were so appealing. He was always smiling. He charmed not only the *behas* (old ladies) in my family but also won the respect of the men with his work ethic and his easy laugh.

Joe spent many hours working with my family, fixing and building things around the house. Every weekend they were either repairing a roof, door, or window or building a house or shed. Joe had a natural talent with a hammer and screwdriver. Much of the time he might have spent with me, he spent making the behas laugh, telling jokes about his life growing up in New Jersey. Joe was very smart. He knew well that the fastest path to my heart was by way of my family.

Even though my family loved Joe, they were surprised when I

accepted his marriage proposal. No one believed I would marry a military man because that meant leaving family and friends … and the island. However, after eight months of courting, we were married in a traditional three-day marriage ceremony, which allowed sufficient time for all of my relatives from the island and beyond to attend.

The first two days of our wedding feast was a non-stop party with constant food, music, and dancing. On the evening of the third day, we were escorted to our honeymoon shack—my relatives and friends singing and laughing all the way. We were exhausted and collapsed in each other's arms, too tired for romance.

Two days following the ceremony, I found myself sitting in the military base air terminal on Guam with Joe. We had had our tearful goodbyes with family and friends, and I was about to take my first airplane ride—one that was to take me away from my home into a completely unknown world. I was not fearful of this new adventure. I was looking forward to it. After the war, I took nothing for granted and loved all of life. I had learned to be open to new possibilities and to look for the good in most every situation. With open-minded anticipation, I wondered where my place would be in my new world.

Before leaving Guam, Joe and I talked about challenges we would encounter on the mainland. We were not worried about the hardship of living on an airman's salary or beginning our life without family. There was only one real challenge: the prejudice that would haunt me on the mainland. Hatred against anything Japanese was very real. I didn't have a drop of Japanese blood, but my Saipanese heritage gave me Asian traits, including my slanted eyes. My skin, which is a much lighter shade than other Guamanians', also made me appear Japanese, not to the Guamanians but to visiting Americans. Many Guamanians had dark brown skin. There had been several occasions on the island after the war that I had been mistaken for Japanese, and I hated it. Before coming to Guam, Joe had witnessed examples of hatred toward Asian people on the mainland. We had reasons to expect hostility.

It was not long before we had our first encounter with an American who hated the Japanese. After the long airplane ride from Guam to California, I was exhausted and a little weak. I learned that although I was not afraid of flying, I suffered terribly from motion sickness. In the air terminal at our first stop in the United States, I was trying to get my bearings and calm my angry stomach when a woman who had been sitting in a nearby chair suddenly stood up after I sat down two chairs from her. I did not realize that she had been watching me and Joe since we had walked into the terminal. Joe was holding my arm, steadying me.

"I cannot believe they let Japs fly on American airplanes!" the woman said with disgust. Joe looked at me.

"How dare you bring one of those women to our country! You married one of those savages?" The woman said, eyeing our wedding rings. "You should have married a good American girl instead of one of those Japanese barbarians."

Joe stood up and opened his mouth to defend me. I touched his arm and motioned for him to sit down. "Please, Joe. She is not bothering me. Please stay with me." Before Joe could respond, his friend Bill, another Air Force airman who was travelling with us, moved to stand between the woman and Joe.

"Bernie is not Japanese. She is from the island of Guam. She was held captive for nearly three years by the Japanese. During the war, they killed many of her family and friends. Leave her alone!"

The woman was surprised at Bill's response. She left but did not apologize.

As much as I tried to forgive the Japanese, I could not and was disgusted to be mistaken for one of them. We knew there would be more encounters like this one. Joe and I thanked Bill, and as always Joe made light of the situation.

"Too bad you could not have found your motion sickness again and vomited on her," Joe said.

"Instead of finding a way to get more out of my stomach, we should put something in it," I said as we unpacked the food that Connie had prepared for us. I smiled as I remembered spending some time with Connie before my wedding. She had flown back to Guam to be my matron of honor. Joe, Bill, and I smiled and we ate the delicious rice and chicken that Connie had cooked for us. Soon we were laughing about the entire episode. We all agreed that Bill was a true friend. He, like Joe, was a newlywed and had received orders to the Air Force base in Massachusetts. His wife was already at his new duty station, waiting for him. He had been on a temporary assignment in Guam shortly after he was married when he met Joe. It did not take long for them to become close friends.

When we arrived in Massachusetts, Joe and I found a small apartment in the same apartment complex as Bill's. We took special care decorating our tiny studio apartment. Joe and I loved to cook and entertain, so we did not wait long to host our first small dinner party. The first dinner guests we invited to our home were Bill and his wife, whom we had not met before. I fixed Joe's favorite Guamanian dish, chicken adobo.

Bill and his wife arrived right on time. I was so shocked when a small woman followed Bill through the door. I could not believe it. Bill's wife was Japanese. He had never said a word about his wife. I could feel the hate filling my heart. I did not want her in my home. Joe greeted her warmly and slapped Bill on the back when Bill introduced his wife, Chong, to Joe and me. I could not say anything to her throughout the evening. After dinner, the men talked and exchanged stories about the latest sports events, politics, and music. Chong and I sat on opposite sides of the room and did not participate in any of the conversation. I think Chong had immediately sensed my discomfort. Two hours passed and it was time for Bill and Chong to leave. They thanked us for dinner and left. After Bill and Chong left, I said, "Joe, I know Bill is your friend, but I cannot have Chong in my home." I was so angry I was shaking. All the hate I felt for the Japanese came rushing back in my head.

"Bernie, I understand how you must feel about Chong, but Bill is our friend. Don't you remember how he defended you at the terminal in San Diego? Chong is an American citizen who was born in California. During the war she and her family were treated terribly. Americans locked them up in concentration camps too, just because they were of Japanese descent. She had nothing at all to do with what the Japanese did to you and your family. She, like you, suffered during the war. It is just as ridiculous for you to hate her as it was for that woman in the terminal to hate you."

"Joe, when I look at her I see the Japanese soldiers."

"But she is not one of the Japanese soldiers. She is just a person, like you and me. She should not be held responsible for the actions of those people from the past."

I stopped talking. I knew he was right but did not know how to stop my rage. I remembered my discussion with Grandmother Lilly about the enemy within and that hate and anger can only lead to more hate and more anger.

Joe and Bill soon received orders for an isolated tour far away from us. This meant that Chong and I both would be left alone. We soon learned that the community of military wives depended on each other for friendship and moral support. I did not hesitate to accept an invitation to attend one of the first get-togethers for the wives. I was eager to learn the ways of Americans and knew the only way to do that was to dive in and socialize.

I arrived at the meeting, which was held at the home of the sergeant in charge of Joe's unit, and was greeted warmly by the sergeant's wife, Susan. There were ten other wives in the room, including Chong, who was sitting in a corner of the living room. I sat in an opposite corner from her.

Susan must have sensed the tension between us and started making small talk. She asked me where I was from. At first, neither Chong nor I said anything. Another one of the wives had brought her mother with her, who was from Massachusetts. As she sat down, she spotted me and Chong. "I can't stay here with two women from the country that killed so many of our men and boys," she said with revulsion. I was so startled by her attitude that I could not say a word.

I was surprised even more when Chong stood up and said, "Bernie is not Japanese. She and I are Americans. My father is from California and my mother was born in Japan. Bernie was held as a prisoner for three years and watched many of her family and friends die at the hands of the Japanese. I lost my only brother in the Battle of Midway, where he was fighting against the Japanese for our country. Don't worry, you don't need to leave because I am not going to stay where I am not wanted." Chong headed for the door.

I finally understood what Joe had been trying to tell me. I did not want to be like the woman from the airport terminal or this angry woman. I did not want to carry the old enemy of hate inside my heart any longer.

"Wait, Chong. I will come with you," I said.

Susan stopped both of us at the door. "There is no reason for either of you to leave. I want you in my home, and if there is anyone in the room who does not like that, they are welcome to leave."

We hesitated but remained, as did all the other women. After that meeting, Chong and I became close friends. We supported each other during our husbands' long tours away and stayed in touch until Chong died in November 1991.

I learned a valuable lesson from my friendship with Chong. Just as I had learned as a child in the concentration camp, the enemies known as hate and prejudice produce only fear and hate. Over the years, I continued to find the good in all people and learned that Grandmother Lilly and Nanan Beha were right: without the enemy of hate inside of me, there was room only for love.

Epilogue

EVEN THOUGH THIS BOOK IS FICTION, ONLY A HANDFUL OF THE stories did not actually take place. A few examples of what really happened include the following:

- Bernie did cut her hair, and doing so saved her life two times.
- Bernie did have her mother's statue of the Virgin Mary in the concentration camp. The statue is displayed in the author's home today.
- The Imperial Japanese Army did drop the first bombs on Guam on December 8, 1941, and captured Guam on December 10, 1941.

- During the Japanese occupation, the people of Guam suffered terrible atrocities, including torture, beheadings, and rape.
- After years of confinement, the people of Guam were also subjected to fierce fighting when U.S. troops recaptured the island in July 1944.
- Guamanians all over the world still celebrate Guam Liberation Day in July.
- The little Catholic church on Sumay was destroyed and only the five-foot cross still stands.
- Thousands of Guamanians were held captive for more than thirty-one months.
- The "comfort house" was a real place.
- The executions took place as described.
- Hundreds of Guamanians, among them members of the Insular Guard, died in captivity.
- The island of Guam was devastated. My mother's hometown, Sumay, was destroyed and not rebuilt. The village of Santa Rita was born nearby; many residents of Sumay moved to Santa Rita.
- Thousands of American soldiers died between 1941 and 1944 either protecting or liberating Guam.
- During the war people across the world did not know how the inhabitants of Guam and other islands in the Pacific suffered. Many are still unaware.
- Thousands of Guamanians survived the war and went on to work with Americans to rebuild, restore, and reclaim their lives and the glory of their island.

Bernie fulfilled her dream of having a large family. She has seven children, twenty-three grandchildren, and thirty great-grandchildren. She worked as a bookkeeper for the federal government and retired after forty years of service. She remains active in the Catholic Church and currently lives with her husband outside Charleston, South Carolina.

Acknowledgements

I AM GRATEFUL TO MANY PEOPLE WHO WERE AN INTEGRAL PART OF my writing *Natural Destiny*. First, I want to thank my mother for sharing her story with me. Without her willingness to tell her story and her encouragement to write it, it would never have come to be. My siblings and I are so blessed to have her in our lives. Thanks also to my brothers and sisters—Joe, Carrie Ann, Betty, Joanne, Victor, and Jerry—for their constant encouragement to write this book. Thanks to my son, Eddie, and my daughter, Connie. They supported me throughout the writing process and told me to trust my dream. They also helped me develop the idea for the book cover. I love my children so much, and each time I see the incredible adults they have become, I beam with pride.

Thanks so much to Cayce Morgan, the founder and owner of the graphic design company Intuitively Artistic. After Connie and Eddie came up with the idea for the book cover, I shared it with Cayce, who took care of the rest.

Thank you also to Destiny, my oldest of my eight grandchildren. Destiny was my first reader. With her input I was able to shape the story you see today.

Thank you to my dear friend Deb Pusillo for all the hours we spent in Starbucks talking about my book and our dreams. In 2010 I knew I needed to attend the Words and Music Conference and so did Deb, who helped me get there. One of the most unselfish people I know, Deb is someone I am proud to call my friend.

Thank you to another dear friend, Lynne LeRoy, who has been such a rock for me, listening to and praying for me. Her strong faith helps sustain me.

Thank you to my friends and family who so graciously agreed to be my test readers: Carol Anderson, Carol Baxley, Amy Carlson, Margaret Edwards, Teresa Herbert, Jeff Hickerson, Donna Jarrell, Connie Lanier, Alice Muller, Deb Pusillo, Janet Smyth, and my parents. I am grateful they took time from their busy schedules to help me craft this book. Their input was invaluable.

Thank you to Lisa Chewning (Write-It-Right). I took an evening writing class at the James Island High School as part of Charleston County's Continuing Education program. The class was one of the best things I have ever done for myself. In the first class when I struggled to say that I was a writer, Lisa said, "Sherry, never apologize for being a writer." It was a simple statement, but after hearing it I allowed myself to write freely. For the following three months I took every free moment and wrote what was to be the bones of the book

There is no way this book would have evolved into this final version had it not been for the love and care of the members of the original Fork Writers' Group. Every Wednesday for more than a year, I met with this group at the Fork Restaurant in Charleston, SC. These wonderful women listened to multiple versions of each chapter and gave valuable feedback. Thank you Fork Writers, especially Wadene August, Christy Bolchoz, Judith Burns, Lisa Chewning, Margaret Edwards, Trish Graf, Nielle Lott, Liz Martinez-Gibson, Jay Roberts, Nina Smith, Wendy Stabler, and Paula Todd-King. A special thank you goes to one member in particular, Janet Smyth. She not only provided weekly input at our meetings but also agreed to read two drafts. Janet has a natural eye for detail, for which I am truly grateful.

Thank you to the Center for Women and all the women I met in the Center's affordable, first-rate writing and marketing classes. This organization does great work to help women develop into who they want to be. My special thanks go to Shari Stauch (www.sharkmarketingco.com), the president of the Center's board of directors. A published author with a successful marketing firm, Shari helps others work toward their dream. I know because she helped me.

Thank you to cj Madigan (www.shoebox-stories.com), who designed the book. In less than three weeks, with cj at the helm, we went from a final draft to a published book. Thank you cj for your hard work and your leadership.

Thank you to my editor, Mary B. Johnston (www.marywordworks.com). From the very beginning, Mary knew we had a deadline and never said it could not be done. She is tireless, remarkable, knowledgeable, and efficient.

Last but not least, my special thanks go to Don, my husband. Since I work full time during the day, there were many nights and weekends that I spent almost all my free time in our home office writing—coming out only to eat and sleep. Don supported me every step of the way. He listened, provided input when I asked, waited, and supported me with everything I wanted or needed to get my book written. I love him forever and a day!

Resources

CENTER MILITARY HISTORY, UNITED STATES ARMY, WASHINGTON, D.C
http://www.history.army.mil/books/wwii/guam/guam77div-fm.htm

GUAMPEDIA, THE ENCYCLOPEDIA OF GUAM
http://guampedia.com/

WAR IN THE PACIFIC
http://www.nps.gov/wapa/index.htm

NAVAL BASE GUAM
http://www.cnic.navy.mil/Guam/AboutUs/History/index.htm

NOTABLE EVENTS IN GUAM'S HISTORY
http://ns.gov.gu/history.html

IMPERIAL JAPANESE ARMY
http://en.wikipedia.org/wiki/
Imperial_Japanese_Navy_of_World_War_II

THE BATTLE OF GUAM
http://en.wikipedia.org/wiki/Battle_of_Guam_(1944)

THE HISTORY OF GUAM
http://en.wikipedia.org/wiki/History_of_Guam

Pictures

CHAPTER 1: LOOKIING BACK
http://en.wikipedia.org/wiki/File:Guam_1941.gif

CHAPTER 2: SUMAY
http://guampedia.com/guam-seal-and-flag/

CHAPTER 3: THE END OF THE WORLD
http://www.nps.gov/history/history/online_books/npswapa/ext-Content/wapa/defense/defense1.htm

CHAPTER 4: SANCTUARY
http://www.nps.gov/history/history/online_books/npswapa/gallery/Guam-2.htm

CHAPTER 5: A PLAN
http://www.flickr.com/photos/robynsnest/12720044/

CHAPTER 6: COPING
http://www.nps.gov/history/history/online_books/npswapa/ext-Content/wapa/defense/defense1.htm

CHAPTER 7:MANENGGON
http://www.123rf.com/photo_8200663_virgin-mary-statue-at-chantaburi-province-thailand.html

CHAPTER 8: HAIR
http://www.nps.gov/history/history/online_books/npswapa/ext-Content/wapa/defense/defense2.htm

CHAPTER 9: WORK
http://www.history.navy.mil/photos/events/wwii-pac/misc-42/dooltl.htm

CHAPTER 10: EXECUTION
http://www.nps.gov/history/history/online_books/npswapa/extContent/Lib/liberation13.htm

CHAPTER 11: DAILY LIFE
http://www.nps.gov/history/history/online_books/npswapa/extContent/Lib/liberation12.htm

CHAPTER 12: BERNIE'S PEOPLE
http://www.nps.gov/history/history/online_books/npswapa/extContent/Lib/liberation32.htm

CHAPTER 13: STARVATION
http://www.nps.gov/history/history/online_books/npswapa/extContent/wapa/encounters/encounters4.htm

CHAPTER 14: DETERMINATION
http://www.nps.gov/history/history/online_books/npswapa/extContent/wapa/guides/first/sec4.htm

CHAPTER 15: TAOTAOMONA
With permission from artist - Raphael Unpingco
http://www.flickr.com/photos/guampedia/4169964091/

CHAPTER 16: FATE AND FAITH
http://www.nps.gov/history/history/online_books/npswapa/extContent/Lib/liberation10.htm

CHAPTER 17: THE ENEMY
http://www.nps.gov/history/history/online_books/npswapa/extContent/usmc/pcn-190-003126-00/sec3.htm

CHAPTER 18: LIBERATION
http://www.ibiblio.org/hyperwar/OnlineLibrary/photos/events/wwii-pac/japansur/js-8g.htm

CHAPTER 19: REUNION
http://www.nps.gov/history/history/online_books/npswapa/gallery/albums/album11/NA_14.htm

CHAPTER 20: DECISIONS
http://www.nps.gov/history/history/online_books/npswapa/extContent/Lib/liberation32.htm

CHAPTER 21: CHOICES
http://www.nps.gov/history/history/online_books/npswapa/extContent/wapa/memorial_wall/index.htm

14847271R00111

Made in the USA
Charleston, SC
04 October 2012